WOMEN
WITH HANDCUFFS

WOMEN WITH HANDCUFFS

LESBIAN COP EROTICA

EDITED BY

SACCHI GREEN

CLEiS
PRESS

Published in the United States by Cleis Press, Inc., 2246 Sixth St., Berkeley, CA 94710.

Printed in the United States.
Cover design: Scott Idleman/Blink
Cover photograph: Damir Spanic/Getty Images
Text design: Frank Wiedemann

First Edition.
10 9 8 7 6 5 4 3 2 1

Trade paper ISBN: 978-1-62778-038-4
E-book ISBN: 978-1-62778-055-1

Contents

INTRODUCTION

What *is* it about lesbian cops that pushes all the right buttons (and some of the deliciously transgressive wrong ones)? It's not just the uniform, with handcuffs and weapons, or the confidence, authority and sense of danger. The intrinsic appeal of women taking on roles that have traditionally been seen as hypermasculine is part of it, of course. To hold their own they need to be hyper-strong, in body, mind and strength of will. That's intensely sexy, for me, at least, and if you've read this far I suspect it is for you, too.

But there's something more as well, an irresistible force that these writers have channeled into fiercely erotic stories of police-women in or out of uniform, on patrol or undercover, in charge or in need of healing, on the case or under the sheets.

The action can be gut-level tough, as in Jove Belle's "Hollis," where anti-terrorism boot camp surges over the edge into BDSM; or heart-wrenching, as in Evan Mora's "A Cop's Wife," when death threats give a keen edge to the need for life-affirming sex;

or quirky as well as steamy when Teresa Noelle Roberts's cop finds a way to maintain respect for her own "Dress Uniform" while indulging her anime-girl lover's cosplay kink.

The settings vary as well, affecting the mood and feel of each piece. Delilah Devlin's cops play their "Only Game in Town" in a southern city that's small without being entirely small-minded. Kenzie Mathews's Alaskan village is a natural place for the mythic "Raven Brings the Light." J. L. Merrow heats up a British town during one "Blazing June," and Cheyenne Blue goes down under to an Australian rain forest for "How Does Your Garden Grow?"

J. N. Gallagher's "Officer Birch" inspires undying passion in a midwestern high school; Lynn Mixon's witness protection marshal finds (and gives) a "Healing Hand" in an unidentified (of course) mountain location; Andrea Dale's "Charity and Splendor" merge in a nice family neighborhood; and Elizabeth Coldwell's handcuffed stripper in "Torn Off a Strip" meets her match on a suburban porch. And in my own story, a state trooper-turned-bodyguard just keeps "Riding the Rails" from Vermont to D.C., with special attention to the roomy handicapped restroom.

Urban scenes range from R. G. Emanuelle's sweet and spicy "Cop at My Door" and Ily Goyanes's "Undercover" hooker who's in way over her head in Miami, to R. V. Raiment's gritty (and lyrical) "Chapel Street Blue" and Annabeth Leong's searing, stirring and ultimately redeeming "A Prayer Before Bed."

The characters, of course, are the real heart and strength of any story. I'm not easily impressed, but these writers did the trick; they walked the fine line between fantasy and believability, without ever slipping into caricature, and gave us fully rounded people, explicit, uncompromising eroticism and their own sizzling visions of the complexity and depth, the strength and vulnerability, and above all the commanding, overwhelming sex appeal of lesbian cops.

They've definitely made me resolve to support my local policewomen.

Sacchi Green
Amherst, Massachusetts

HOLLIS

Jove Belle

Sweat rolled down Jen's back and saturated the waistband of her federal issue gym shorts. Her heart pounded as she gulped air. She'd been warned. Squad mates who'd previously attended the FBI anti-terrorism training session told her it wouldn't be all book learning. They hadn't, however, prepared her for the sadistic instructor who'd made it her mission to make Jen's lungs bleed.

Seven miles for fuck's sake. When she chased perps, which wasn't very often, they ran for a block or two. Half-a-mile, tops. They did not race full out through the woods, over trees, splashing through streams for seven fucking miles. She was here to learn how to catch terrorists, not Bambi.

For now, though, she'd settle for catching her breath.

"Move it, people." Special Agent Hollis smiled. "Get a drink of water and let's go. The American people don't want to waste their tax dollars paying you to breathe."

Jen pictured the instructor in a leather corset snapping a whip at their heels. It wasn't an entirely unpleasant image, even if the timing was crap. Forget the fact that they were surrounded by Jen's classmates, or that she didn't even know the instructor's first name—Special Agent Hollis was far too long for an exhaled moan. The brutal, slipping-toward-middle-age truth was she was too damn tired to enjoy the fantasy.

"You're drooling again." Reeva, Jen's twenty-something blonde roommate, handed her a cup of water and collapsed on the grass next to her.

Jen swiped her hand over her mouth and chin just in case Reeva's observation was literal.

"Thanks." She took a long drink, then poured the rest over her head. If the ice-cold water didn't cool her down, nothing would.

"Show of hands, people." Special Agent Hollis dangled a pair of handcuffs from her finger. "Who here has actually cuffed a perp?"

Jen raised her hand reluctantly. At close to forty, she was probably the only person in the group to have done a lot of things, but that didn't mean she wanted to be singled out. She had the sinking feeling that with the admission, she had volunteered for something.

"Really? Lassiter's the only one?" Hollis raised a brow and snapped the cuffs through the air to Jen, the chrome winking in the sunlight. "Bring your roommate with you."

"Great," Reeva mumbled under her breath as she followed Jen to the front. "I get to be strapped to your work-experience ass."

A trickle of sweat threatened to fall into Jen's eyes, and she hiked up her shirt to wipe her brow. The cool breeze against her skin was a revelation. She took her shirt off completely, used it to towel her hair to spikey submission, then tossed it to the side while she waited direction. She doubted the FBI would approve of her change in wardrobe, but she wasn't a federal employee so she figured she could push it. What's the worst that could happen? Special Agent Hollis would punish her? A thrill ran over her at the thought.

Hollis's gaze lingered on Jen's abs. The run may have turned her into a sweaty, heaving wreck, but what she lacked in cardiovascular endurance, she more than made up for in muscular definition. She tightened her stomach. If Hollis wanted to stare at her for the remainder of class, Jen was fine with that.

"Lassiter, pretend you're an agent and cuff her."

"How 'bout I just be a detective and do it anyway." Jen turned to Reeva without waiting for a response. "Turn around, hands on the back of your head, fingers interlaced."

Like most people, Reeva did as she was told, and Jen snapped the handcuffs home on one wrist, guided both arms down behind Reeva's back, and secured the other side. She spun her around and stood, hand reflexively positioned low on Reeva's bicep. She didn't actually think Reeva would try to run away, but you can't undo almost twenty years of training and practice.

"Good." Hollis unlocked Reeva. "This time trade positions."

"Really?" Being restrained wasn't new to Jen, but she only yielded to those who proved worthy. So far, Reeva hadn't demonstrated the appropriate amount of strength to make Jen willing to slip into that role.

Hollis regarded Jen, her face placid, almost bored. "Really."

"Turn around, and put your hands behind you?" Reeva sounded uncertain. Until that point, the prescribed script had been words on a test, and she struggled to get them in the right order.

"Yeah, about that," Jen took a step back, "I don't think so."

"Huh?" Reeva reached for Jen's wrist and Jen slapped her hand away.

"Not everyone goes down easily." Jen smiled at Reeva and took another step away. She felt bad for making things harder for her roommate, but not bad enough to acquiesce.

"No, not everyone does." Hollis spoke from behind, her lips close to Jen's ear, her breath hot and teasing against Jen's neck. "But eventually, everybody goes down."

Before Jen could spin around, Hollis twisted her arm behind her, pressing her fingers high between her shoulder blades, and kicked the back of her knee, forcing her to the ground. Jen landed hard, her face muffled in the grass. "Fuck," she groaned.

Hollis twisted the arm a little higher and pressed her knee into Jen's back. The sudden pressure was sharp and wicked. Jen gasped, relishing the aggressive touch. It'd been forever since someone had commanded her attention through brute force, and the sensation was delicious.

The cutting edge of metal bit into Jen's wrists when Special Agent Hollis snapped the cuffs in place, cinching them down tighter than any law enforcement agency allowed. Jen struggled, pushing up against Hollis, knowing that she couldn't get away, but desperate to test her boundaries. Hollis shoved her down roughly, mashing Jen's cheek into the sod. The rich earthy scent of grass soothed her, a direct counterpoint to the harsh command Hollis issued. "Stay down."

"Yes, ma'am." Jen stopped squirming and held her body rigid, the urge to obey too deeply engrained to suppress. She averted her eyes, out of habit rather than need. She hadn't been able to see more than a glimpse of Hollis since she'd forced her to the ground.

"Good girl." Hollis rubbed her thumb lightly over the skin just above the handcuffs—a touch too intimate to be unintentional.

Jen remained facedown for the remainder of the training

session. By the time Special Agent Hollis helped her to her feet and removed the cuffs, Jen's hands were numb and her panties were soaked. She hoped her classmates couldn't see just how excited the encounter had made her but doubted she was hiding it well. And, at that point, she would have done anything the instructor asked, regardless of the audience.

Hollis held out Jen's shirt. "Wait in my office."

Jen ached to rub the feeling back into her wrists and hands, work the stiffness out of her back and shoulders. Instead, she took the proffered shirt with a curt nod and turned toward the building without a word, leaving Special Agent Hollis behind to dismiss the other students.

She debated pulling her shirt on as she walked and opted against it. Since Hollis didn't specify if she wanted her dressed or not, she ran the chance of being wrong either way, but if the decision were left to Jen, as it apparently was at the moment, she preferred fewer clothes for their meeting, not more.

The office was easy to find, listed on the directory along with countless other Special Agent so-and-so instructors. Her entire name was printed on the nameplate next to the door. Special Agent Beverly Hollis. Jen smiled. Now she knew the instructor's first name, a name that she planned to be moaning later, whether under her own efforts or with help.

When Jen turned the knob, she found the door unlocked. She folded her shirt and laid it on a wooden chair just inside the door. Should she remove the rest of her clothing? No, she decided as she dropped to her knees midway between the door and the desk. She faced the door, clasped her hands together behind her back and settled in to wait for Hollis's arrival. She kept her gaze focused on the square of carpet directly in front of her. The temptation to explore the office was too great. If she allowed herself to glance around, she'd be up and snooping through the desk in moments. She did not want to be caught in that position.

When she heard the soft rattle-click of someone turning the knob, it could have been minutes or hours later. She'd learned long ago to surrender to the moment, allowing time to flow around her without trying to capture it or gauge the duration. She straightened her posture, wanting to impress Special Agent Hollis.

"I see you're capable of obedience." Hollis skimmed one finger over Jen's shoulders and up, teasing the surface of her hair without coming close enough to actually touch it. Without warning, she gripped a handful of Jen's short locks and forced her head back, demanding eye contact. "You are well trained."

Jen did not respond. Speaking without permission was dangerous. Not that she minded pushing buttons; she just liked to know the results before jumping in. Until she learned Hollis's proclivities, she would err on the side of caution.

"You can speak."

"Thank you." Jen tried to avert her gaze again, and Hollis gave a sharp tug on her hair. Jen wouldn't need a third lesson. Hollis liked to be watched.

Hollis released her hair. "Stand."

Jen rose fluidly, her movements graceful in spite of not moving for so long, first facedown on the field, then kneeling here on the carpet. She'd spent hours alone practicing how to move from feet to knees and back again. She wanted to be beautiful, and she'd been told many times over that her efforts had paid off.

Hollis circled behind Jen, easing her nails beneath the edge of Jen's sports bra. She snapped the elastic across her back and said, "Strip."

As Jen removed her remaining articles of clothing and folded them carefully, Hollis pulled several items out of her filing cabinet and placed them on her desk in a line. A sleek wooden hairbrush, teak perhaps, a set of clamp-style paper clips, a manila folder, and a child's school ruler, wooden with a metal edge.

"Stand two steps from the desk, eyes on me, bend at the waist and grasp the edge."

Jen followed the directions precisely, measuring out two steps before moving into position. She kept her head up, unsure if she should maintain eye contact or follow Hollis's hands as they worked to remove the metal strip from the side edge of the ruler. The steady, sure movements of her hands won out, as Jen found herself captivated, imagining the sting of the wood against her backside.

When Hollis finished removing the thin line of metal, she returned it to the desk and selected the manila folder next. She relaxed, sinking into her chair as she read, "Jennifer May Lassiter, homicide detective, North Precinct Portland, Oregon. Shot twice in the line of duty." Hollis looked up, her eyes searching Jen's body for evidence to support the information in the file. Her gaze lingered on the rough scar on Jen's shoulder, then continued the search of her body. She wouldn't find the one just below Jen's left breast as long as Jen remained angled over the desk. "Decorated as a hero for stopping a robbery in progress and a second time for safely negotiating the release of a family taken hostage in their own home." She stopped reading, waiting for Jen to fill in the details.

Jen held her gaze, but didn't speak. That day had been a horrible, crazy mix-up of luck and coincidence. The only reason she was here instead of dead was because the man's pistol jammed, and she was able to tackle him before he cleared the chamber. The barrel had been pointed straight at her chest—covered in patrol officer blue—when he pulled the trigger. At her close proximity, it would have done more than leave another scar to be cataloged in a file.

She'd been promoted to detective a week later. Her second

promotion to detective investigator came after she brought in a serial rapist who had terrorized the St. John's area for months. After that, she requested the transfer to Homicide, where the victims didn't cry when she found them.

Nothing in their exchange so far permitted Hollis to hear Jen's accounting of that part of her life, and if she continued to stare at Jen, entitlement and demand on her face, Jen would end the scene and leave. She wanted to get laid, not head fucked.

Jen eased her grip on the desk, already mentally removing herself from the room. As she was about to straighten and retrieve her clothing, Hollis finally spoke.

"Everything in here reads like a chief's wet dream." Hollis closed the file and set it next to the ruler, then picked up the metal clips. "So why are you down here being such a pain in the ass for me?"

"I…" Jen flexed her fingers, muscles aching as she renewed her grasp. What could she say in her own defense? What would be good enough? "I'm sorry." She lowered her gaze, unable to keep her eyes forward during the apology. It wouldn't be enough for Hollis, she was sure, but it was the best she could offer.

"You're sorry?" Hollis was on her feet and by Jen's side quick enough to make Jen flinch. "You disrupt my class, embarrass your classmate, and that's all you have to say for yourself?" She spoke low and harsh in Jen's ear, her hand bouncing the metal clips up, just barely losing contact, then grasping them tight, her fingers loose and steady. Over and over. The rhythmic clicking lulled Jen.

"Umm…" Jen wanted to speak eloquently, to defend herself. All she could do was watch the flash of metal between Hollis's fingers.

Hollis leaned closer, her lips brushing against Jen's neck, just below her ear. "Sorry isn't enough. There are consequences for that type of behavior in my classroom." She sucked Jen's earlobe between her teeth and bit down hard.

Hollis pressed her fingertips against Jen's shoulder, forcing her upright. She kissed and sucked her way down Jen's chest, taking first one nipple into her mouth, a barely there open-mouthed kiss, then the other. "Your breasts are remarkable." As she spoke, she gripped both nipples between her thumbs and forefingers and squeezed.

Jen gasped, fisting her palms at her side to keep from grabbing Hollis and pulling her closer. The pressure increased steadily until all Jen could think about, all that mattered, was the urgent thrum of hot, lustful energy running from her breasts to her cunt. Her knees trembled and she felt herself slipping. She forced herself upright and braced herself. She would not fall over.

Just as the pressure reached the hard-enough-to-make-her-come level, Hollis released her. Before Jen could orient herself, return to a semi-normal state, Hollis slipped a clamp over her left nipple, then her right. The pressure rocketed, too painful, too decadent, too immediate, too jarring, too delicious, too... everything. Jen wanted more and she wanted less. Unable to decide, she whimpered and leaned closer to Hollis.

"I want you to make me come." Hollis slid out of her shorts and panties as she led Jen around the desk. "Then I'll decide on a suitable punishment for you." She reclined into her chair, forcing Jen to her knees and guiding her head between her legs in one smooth motion.

Jen eased her hands over Hollis's thighs, working her way up and inward, delighted that she was allowed to touch.

"Ah-ah, hands behind your back." She rapped the ruler over Jen's knuckles.

"I'm sorry." Jen slipped her tongue between Hollis's lips, her words muffled. She fought to keep her balance as she stroked and swirled, experimenting with pressure and motion. She was determined to make Hollis forget her own name.

Hollis gripped the back of her head, the constant weight of her hand holding Jen steady. Jen thrust her tongue into Hollis, pushing as deep as she could, reaching to find Hollis's threshold for pleasure. She retracted and thrust again, building a steady rhythm that Hollis matched, her hips jutting into Jen's face. Jen wanted to grip Hollis around the waist, drag her close, pin her down, and tongue-fuck her until she came.

The tugging pressure on Jen's scalp increased sharply in sync with the rising volume of Hollis's praise. "Fuck...god...damn." Over and over, the same three words that started as a low, barely-there whisper grew into a proud, desperate mantra.

Jen dragged her tongue up, applying direct pressure to Hollis's clit for the first time. She grazed it with her teeth, then sucked it hard between her lips, flicking the tip of her tongue over the tight bundle.

Hollis gripped Jen's head tighter, her fingers tangled in her hair, pulling and pushing at the same time. Hollis tensed, perfectly still, yet shaking from the strain as her body tightened. She teetered there on that edge, body quaking, until Jen couldn't take it any more. Fuck obedience. She slammed two fingers into Hollis's cunt, fucking her hard and fast.

"Jesus...fuck...fuck." Hollis buckled into the chair and tugged Jen up by her hair, covering her mouth in a demanding, invading kiss. "Damn, you're good at that."

As quickly as the kiss began, it ended. Hollis tugged on both nipple clamps, shooting fire to Jen's center. She almost collapsed in Hollis's lap.

"I want you on the floor, face down, ass up. Now." Hollis's voice held none of the languid recovery Jen expected. Her recuperation time was record fast.

As Jen moved into position, Hollis shoved the cushion from her chair under Jen's head.

"Keep your hands behind your back this time, or I'll put the cuffs back on." She took a set from her top drawer and set them heavily on the desk. "I have a hobby that you are likely unaware of."

Jen could hear Hollis moving around as she spoke, and she struggled to keep her head down. What else could she possibly have in her office to use on Jen? Either the ruler or the hairbrush would work nicely.

"I like to ride." Hollis's smile infused her voice, and Jen would have worried if given enough time. "English style."

A sharp crack from, presumably, Hollis's riding crop tore into Jen's rear end, and she bit her lip to keep from crying out. A second and third quickly followed.

"Feel free to count if it helps." Two more rapid strokes. "Or cry if you need to."

"Six." Jen grinded her teeth together as another sharp blow caught her low enough to sting her pussy lips.

Jen counted fifteen before Hollis stopped. The cool counterpoint of Hollis's hand as she comforted the reddened skin relaxed Jen, and a tear slipped from her eye.

"So beautiful." Hollis's voice was reverent and soft as she massaged Jen's ass, alternating between gripping and pulling, and gliding softly. "You were splendid."

Hollis stretched Jen's cheeks apart and a jolt of cool air hit her anus, followed almost immediately by a slick, probing tongue. Hollis pressed into Jen, rimming her, as her hands continued to knead the abused flesh. Jen squeezed her muscles tight, all of them, her fingernails digging into her palms, her toes digging into the hard tile. Her nipples dragged against the floor, amping up the fire from the clamps, as she strained against Hollis's tongue.

One last swipe and Hollis sat back on her haunches, still holding Jen's cheeks open. Jen held herself rigid, fighting against the feeling of being exposed, vulnerable.

"God, I wish I had a strap-on here. I'd fuck your ass so hard you'd come for weeks."

Before the words could cool in the air, before Jen's pussy could stop clenching from the promise, Hollis pushed three fingers into her cunt, so hard and so deep Jen wondered if it really was a strap-on. She set a fast steady pace, increasing to four fingers before Jen was ready, and the stretching pressure-pain almost made Jen come instantly. She wasn't allowed yet, and she gritted her teeth and waited for permission.

Hollis grasped Jen's hair, tugging her upright, flush against her, back to front, as she continued to fuck her. The new angle and increasing urgency brought Jen closer to the edge until she was staring down, trying not to fall into the vast chasm before her. She was barely hanging on, her grasp on solid ground tenuous and failing fast.

Hollis released Jen's hair and wrapped her arm around her chest, toying with her nipples, one after the other, not letting either rest for more than a second before returning her attention to it. Then, blessedly, she licked the length of Jen's neck, still thrusting hard inside her cunt.

"Do you want to come?"

Jen's shoulders burned and ached, and her fingers itched to dig into the flesh of Hollis's belly. Her head swam, furling and dark.

"Answer me." Hollis tugged on one of the clamps, pulling and squeezing it tighter. "Do you want to come?"

Yes...yes...god, yes. Jen couldn't form the words. Her body was on fire, originating in her pussy and burning outward. She licked her lips. "Y..." She licked them again. "Yes, please, yes."

She begged and cried, unable to think beyond the pounding fist in her cunt and the lightning sharp pressure on her nipples.

Hollis released her hold on the clamp, leaving it in place, but no longer adding to the pain. She moved her hand swiftly to Jen's mound, circling her clit with one soft, determined finger. "You can." She bit down on the meaty flesh of Jen's shoulder as she spoke.

Jen froze. Permission. She opened herself to the pressure in her cunt, her clit, her nipples, and sharp tear of teeth at her pulse point. The dark, blurry edges of her vision overpowered the light and she surrendered, falling head first into the abyss.

When Jen came to, Hollis was dressed and staring at her intently. The polished leather of her riding boots sat in stark contrast to the dull linoleum tiles. She tucked the crop under her arm, a tight, secret smile gracing her lips.

"Tomorrow," she said as she turned on her heel and headed out the door, "try not to disrupt my class again."

The door closed with a solid, final click, and Jen roused herself enough to begin getting dressed. Her body felt battered and spent, but all other evidence of their encounter—the clamps, the ruler, the never-used hairbrush, even the pillow—was gone. She pulled her shirt over her head, taking inventory of the tender and sore places.

Hollis was right; tomorrow Jen would be the model student. But the next day, or perhaps the day after, when her body had recovered…well, that remained to be seen.

Jen slipped out of Special Agent Beverly Hollis's office and took one final glance around the room before closing the door. She wasn't too worried about the details of the room. She would be back again soon enough.

ONLY GAME IN TOWN

Delilah Devlin

I wondered why I'd bothered changing out of my uniform before hitting the bar. Back in the city, the department had strict rules about drinking in uniform. Here, a circle of black uniforms sat crowded around the table in the far corner, cold beers sweating on the scarred wood.

Lonny James caught sight of me and waved me over. "Make room, guys."

He said guys, but there was another female among them: Officer Brown, the bicycle cop who patrolled up and down Main Street in little black bike shorts during shopping hours.

I gave her a nod, then glanced around the table. Lonny pulled out the chair beside him without rising. I sank into it gratefully and accepted the beer he slid my way.

"So how was your first day?"

I shrugged. Boring might sound rude, like a big city cop telling the rest of them their jobs were cakewalks. "It was okay, I guess."

"Get any looks?"

"What do you mean?"

"We aren't used to female cops here."

My glance swung toward Office Brown whose lips pressed into a thin line.

"You've already got one," I murmured.

"Yeah, but..." Lonny wasn't the sharpest tool in the shed and apparently had to think a minute about how to respond when he thought everyone should already know. "She's on a bike."

What an idiot.

I gave a soft laugh, rolled my eyes at Brown and sucked down foam as the men on my shift began to talk about their interesting day.

Lonny's story was the best. He'd intervened between two yard archrivals over a dispute about a sycamore that dropped its pods on the wrong side of a fence. Lonny might not have been all that sharp, but his slow, drawling recounting of how he'd faced off against men armed with a chain saw and a rake had everyone chuckling, including me.

Lonny's gaze dropped to my mouth. "You're pretty when you smile," he whispered.

I arched an eyebrow, suddenly uncomfortable because his thigh was pushing against mine.

I slipped a pen from my purse, out of sight of the others, and jabbed his thigh.

He jumped, cussing loudly, but when the others glanced his way, he said, "Caught my toe under the chair."

He wore steel-toed boots. Like I said, not the brightest light-bulb.

When he settled again, he scooted his chair away. "If I'd known you swung that way," he muttered loudly, "I'd have suggested you take the seat next to Brown."

"Thanks for the suggestion," I said, picking up my drink and walking around the table, aware that all eyes in the bar were on me, and everyone was drawing the same conclusion.

I sat beside Officer Brown, giving her only a quick glance. I didn't want to assume a damn thing. "He always such a dick?" I muttered.

She laughed and held out her hand. "Ramona, and yeah, he thinks he's a stud because he has a badge."

"Cathy." I offered a smile along with my hand. "Glad it wasn't just me."

The officer on the other side of her shook his head. "Don't pay him any mind. He's the sheriff's nephew, and Horace knows good and well he's an idiot."

"We're a little light on the formalities here," Ramona said, eyeing my street clothes. "And they should have assigned you a sponsor—someone to show you the ropes."

"Really?"

"Sheriff probably didn't want to assign one of the married guys because their wives wouldn't like it. You're too pretty. And he couldn't assign Lonny, well, because he's…"

"An idiot."

We shared a grin. I liked the way her smile pulled up the corners of her eyes, slanting them, betraying a drop of Asian blood mixed with the glorious Creole that painted her skin a lovely dark cream.

"So, why didn't he give me you?" I said slowly, holding her gaze.

She blinked and a flush colored her cheeks. "He didn't want you to be offended."

I nodded my understanding. My instincts hadn't lied. "Can I request you?"

"There's not a lot you can't figure out for yourself," she said, stirring a fingertip in the top of her mixed drink.

"That mean you're not interested?" I asked under my breath, wanting to keep our conversation on the down low.

Her eyes widened, and her glance slid away.

I blew out a breath and looked away—into her friend's narrowed glare. I wondered if I had her figured all wrong and he was her boyfriend. Or maybe I'd just come on too strong. But I'm not the kind of girl to let a good thing slip away, not if I can help it.

I took another gulp of my beer, trying to figure out how to exit now that I'd shown my ass to everyone.

Chairs scraped. I glanced up to see the men rising, stretching out their arms and sharing teasing jibes as they prepared to leave.

"Welcome to Canaan," the guy sitting beside Ramona said. He lifted a brow at Ramona, and paused, but she stayed seated. He left with the others.

"That wasn't at all obvious," she muttered.

I wrinkled my nose. "I know how to clear a room."

She gave a scoffing laugh. "It wasn't about your bad behavior. Jonesy was giving us time alone to get to know each other. He didn't think you'd want to out yourself your first damn day. It's a small town. And this is the Bible Belt."

"It worry you? Them knowing?"

"Only if it bothers you."

I smiled, relieved I hadn't blown it. "Fact is, I hoped I'd get a chance to talk to you alone. And I could give a shit whether they're disappointed that I don't *swing* their way."

Ramona's lips pressed into a thin line.

I couldn't tell if she was disapproving of my forwardness or trying to hide a smile.

She cleared her throat. "Most of them are pretty decent—so long as we're not in their face about it."

I nodded and sat back in my chair, crossing one jeans-clad leg over the other. "You dating anyone?"

"Around…" She shrugged. "No one special. You?"

"Same."

Shoving her drink away, she planted an elbow on the table and leaned closer. "Look, you're new. I don't jump in and out of bed with every available dyke just because there are too damn few of us here."

"And I'm not hitting on you because you're the only game in town. Besides, I didn't ask you to sleep with me."

She raised an eyebrow.

"Okay, I want to, but I'll give you a chance to know me first." Sensing I'd pushed her far enough, I rose, dropped folded bills on the table to tip the waitress, and held out her chair. She stood up, smiling but looking a little uncomfortable at the attention we drew.

We parted at the door, exchanging nods, and I headed home. Regrettably, alone.

The next few days were a little strained around the guys. Word got around. Sly glances followed me everywhere. But since I didn't rise to any of their innuendos, the excitement faded and they found someone else to hound.

This day, I'd parked my car at the Stop 'n' Go. It might be small-town Louisiana, but bandits still preferred the ease of a quickie robbery when they were low on cash. The store had been hit twice in the past six months, and the sheriff had promised a "presence" to the owner. So, in between calls, I parked in the hot sun at the edge of the parking lot, running my AC with the window open to ease the humidity inside the vehicle.

The whir of spokes catching the wind whizzed by my car.

Little black shorts hugging a nicely rounded backside caught my attention.

Ramona halted at the edge of the curb next to the shop's front door and eased off her helmet. Sweat stained the center of her back, and her hair lay in wet, tangled spikes around her head. She glanced my way and gave me a smile that set my heart beating faster, then entered the store.

I opened my car door, dumped the fresh cup of coffee I'd bought just a few minutes before and headed inside.

"Back so soon?" Dolores asked from her seat behind the counter.

I gave a quick glance around the aisles but didn't find my quarry. "That cup went right through me," I said, making my way to the restroom in the back.

Once the door swung shut behind me, I quietly locked it.

A toilet flushed. The stall door opened. Ramona stepped out and her eyes widened. "Didn't hear you come in, Cath."

"I won't keep you long."

She walked to the sink, soaped up and cleansed her hands, then used a paper towel to wipe the sweat from her face. "What is it you want?"

I leaned against the bathroom door and folded my arms over my chest. "You said we should take some time to know each other, but that's never gonna happen if you're avoiding me."

She met my glance in the mirror. Challenge glittered in her golden brown eyes. "Is that what you think I'm doing? Why'd I come here when I could have chosen a dozen other businesses to stop in?"

I raised a brow. "Maybe because it's public and you could say you weren't avoiding me and get away with it?"

She grunted, her lips twisting. "Again, what is it you want?"

This wasn't going well. Again, I felt like I had two left feet.

"How about a yes or no?" I blurted. "Wanna go out?"

She gave a feminine grunt. "No."

The disappointment cut, but I nodded, firmed my chin and began to turn.

"There's not anywhere in public we can *go* together, Cath. The sheriff wouldn't like it if we paraded a date. But I'd like you to come over for dinner."

"Your place?" I said, forcing the words past a tightened throat.

"Yeah. Tonight." She sauntered forward and tucked her fingers under the sharp edges of my buttoned collar. Her hand twisted, cinching it around my throat and pulling me down.

I'd kissed women before. Even kissed a few men. This was hotter than any of those—even with two layers of Kevlar between our chests.

Her mouth smoothed over mine, then suctioned. Her lips were thick and juicy, her tongue rimming me. I waited, not charging in, and was rewarded when her tongue pushed against mine. Just a touch, and then it was gone. I tasted mint. She had to taste the coffee I'd guzzled all day.

She leaned back, her mouth open and air gusting as she licked her lips. "Tonight."

She strode past me. I heard the snick of the lock as she opened it. The door whooshed closed.

"*Oh, fuck.*"

That night, I strolled up the sidewalk, wondering if what I wore would please her. I didn't want to make it seem like I'd gone to too much effort in case she wasn't that into me, but she didn't need to know that most of my clothes were strewn across my bed because I hadn't been able to make up my mind until the last moment.

I wore a short, black skirt. Not something I was completely comfortable wearing, but I have nice, well-toned legs, my best asset actually, and I wanted her to notice. The T-shirt I chose was tight and casual with a zombie on the front and the word "brainz..." underneath it. Not sexy, but I hoped the skirt would do the trick. Metallic black sandals completed the outfit.

If things didn't heat up, she wouldn't have to know I'd decided underwear was too much work.

Before I reached the front door, it swung open. I groaned inside, or maybe it wasn't as quiet as I thought, because she grinned. She wore a gauzy dress, one of those Mexican cotton things that followed every curve of her slender body. Completely feminine. Completely delicious. And she was naked underneath it. I could tell because the light from the entry hall shone straight through it.

My gaze raked down, then up.

Her smile was wide and cheeky when I finally reached her face. "Not so bad yourself," she said, her eyelids dipping as she traced the length of my legs. "I like an edgy girl."

I glanced down at the zombie. "It's my favorite T-shirt."

She cupped my breast and rubbed my nipple. "It's soft. I can tell you wear it often."

I pushed her through the door and slammed it behind us. "Don't you care what your neighbors think?"

Her grin was relaxed and infectious. "WWE's on. They won't notice a thing not happening on their TVs tonight." She pinched the front of my shirt and turned, pulling me through her house. We crossed the living room and headed straight for the kitchen.

"Beer or wine?" she asked, finally releasing me. "I also mix a mean margarita."

"Beer's fine."

She snagged one from the fridge for me and picked up a half-full wineglass from the counter, then led me back into the living room. The fight played on the TV, but the sound was turned down.

"Why bother if you can't hear it?" I asked just to start a conversation. I was nervous and horny, and my hands were sweating.

"I wasn't all that interested in the fight, and I wanted to be able to hear your car." She curled up at the end of the sofa, her feet under her.

I sat stiffly, wanting to tug her legs toward me and shove up her dress. Instead I drew on my beer, hoping it would cool the heat simmering inside me.

"I heard you had to go to Schwieg's today," she said over the rim of her glass. Her eyes sparkled with humor.

Mention of the farmer made my lips twitch. "Have to admit that was my very first pig call."

"Your virgin pig call?" she said, laughing softly. "Have any trouble?"

I rolled my eyes. "Pigs are damn mean. There were three of us trying to corral a big boar back into his pen."

"A big boar? They can be dangerous."

"He didn't stand a chance against my Taser."

Her eyes widened and laughter exploded. "No! You Tasered a pig?"

I shrugged, my grin stretching. "What the hell else could I do?"

She wiped tears from her eyes. "Bet Schwieg was ready to shoot you."

"I still had the Taser in my hand," I said dryly. "He was polite."

She chuckled softly. "Wish I could have seen that."

I leaned back against the couch, curling a leg beneath me so I could turn my body toward her. "So, why are you on the bike?

They stick you there because you're a girl?"

"I asked for it. I like the exercise. I get to know the folks really well. Especially the kids. It's why they made me the D.A.R.E. officer at the school. I'm good with them."

I shuddered. "Sorry, I can't see me wearing those shorts. Everybody'd be staring at my ass."

"You stared at mine. And I didn't mind a bit."

I shrugged again, a blush heating my cheeks.

Ramona reached across the top of the sofa to pull a lock of my hair. She twisted it around her finger. "So why'd you leave Houston?"

I liked that she'd made the first move. That she was trying to make me comfortable. "I knew I wasn't going to get off the streets, and I'd had one too many close calls. I'm not all that into adrenaline."

She nodded. "I worked in San Antonio before coming here. I moved there with my boyfriend to go to school but dropped out after two years and applied to the academy. As soon as my contract was up, I headed back here. I like the pace."

"What happened to the boyfriend?"

Ramona wrinkled her nose. "We didn't work."

I nodded my understanding. I hadn't always known what I was either.

Ramona flashed me a sultry look with her pretty brown eyes, then set aside her wineglass.

I drew on my beer and straightened, knowing she'd had enough of small talk.

She stretched out her legs in front of her on the cushions and inched up her skirt.

When the hem barely covered the best parts, I groaned. "Enough, already!"

She laughed and curled her finger, inviting me closer.

My beer slammed on the coffee table, and I came up on my knees on the big couch, bent over her and pushed up the hem of her blue dress to uncover her pussy.

Her bush was trimmed, a narrow black stripe that hugged the edges of her tawny lips. I scraped a fingernail over the edge of her fluff, enjoying the feel of the bristly tips.

She raised her leg and hooked her ankle over the top of the sofa, opening herself, inviting me closer. "It's okay to do more. I promise I don't bite."

I brushed the bristles again and bent toward her pussy, drawing in the scent of her sex and a hint of an exotic perfume, something that smelled like incense. "I love the way you smell," I said softly.

"It's patchouli oil. You like it?"

I nodded and leaned closer, rubbed my nose on the bare skin of her labia, then licked her there.

She groaned and a hand reached down. Her fingers combed my hair and tugged me closer. "I've been dreaming of you tonguing me, Cath. Eating me out."

"I won't disappoint," I said, giving her a wink. Then I inserted my thumb between her folds and scraped it upward, lifting the thin hood that hid her clit. It was swollen and red. I latched onto it with my lips and licked and sucked it until her hips began to rock.

Slipping my hands under her ass, I tilted her toward me, burrowing in, my tongue stroking her inner folds, then sliding deeper for a taste. Moisture greeted me and I drew one hand from under her firm ass and plunged two fingers inside her while I worked her clit.

Her moans grew louder. Her fingernails raked my scalp. I fucked her with three digits and scraped my teeth over her hard little knot, then bit—gently—but enough to shock her into an orgasm.

Her body vibrated and she gave a thin, keening wail while her hips pumped, fucking my fingers, slamming against my mouth.

When her frantic movements slowed, I kissed her inner thighs and lifted my face.

Her smile was strained, her tawny cheeks reddened. Her mouth was swollen as though she'd bitten her lips, and I climbed over her to rest between her spread thighs.

I cupped a cheek and kissed her, stroking her tongue to give her back her flavors, then nuzzled beside her ear while I waited for her breathing to even out.

Ramona smoothed a hand over my back. "I have toys," she whispered.

I dragged in a deep breath, glad we weren't done. "Got a dildo?"

"I have a two-headed one. We can fuck each other with it, if you like..."

I grinned down at her, then rolled off the sofa and stripped away my T-shirt and skirt.

She sat on the edge of the sofa and palmed my buttocks, leaning forward to lick my pussy.

The sight of her dark head between my legs, the feel of her slippery tongue and dainty fingers sliding up inside me, made my belly tighten and moisture ooze down my thighs.

I braced my legs apart, giving her room to explore for a minute or two, and then I pulled her hair to make her stop. "That dildo," I said, breathless now and so horny I felt on the edge of violence.

She rose slowly, rubbing her small breasts on my belly then letting the spiked tips scrape mine.

I pinched a nipple, pulled it, then let it go. "Move it, Brown."

She bit her lower lip and glanced at me from underneath her eyelashes. "Gonna Taser me if I don't move fast enough?"

"Only if that gets you off," I said, reaching around to smack her ass.

She chuckled. "You get mean when you're horny."

"I've been wet for a week just thinking about doing you. It's not nice to tease."

She darted off, running down the hall toward her bedroom. I followed, right on her ass, caught her when she reached the bed and slammed her down face first on the comforter. I crawled over her, straddled her rounded butt, bent to lick her neck and give her teasing bites on her shoulders.

Giggling, she fought to roll over, but I was bigger, stronger—more determined. I slid lower and licked down her spine until I reached her ass.

I trailed my fingers down the crevice and paused to circle her tiny rear hole.

Her breath hitched. "Toys. Under the bed."

I smiled and backed off, ready to stop playing and get down to the serious business of her fucking her silly.

She rolled to her belly and lay there as I slid off the bed and burrowed under it for her "treasure chest."

The plastic container was filled with vibrators, clamps and glossy hard plastic and gel dildos in a range of sizes. I chose the one she'd mentioned, the one she seemed to be most eager to use. It was long, thick, firm and yet flexible enough to curve with my hands. I made a U-shape and held it up.

Her eyebrows rose.

"On your knees, Brown."

She didn't hesitate, coming up on her knees and spreading them when I held one end, pointing it toward her pussy. I fed it inside her, pushing in then pulling it out, working it deeper and deeper until she leaned on a hand and rocked her hips forward and back to fuck it.

Then I moved in closer, sat on a pillow and opened my legs wide. I leaned back on both hands. "Feed it into me, baby. Fuck me with it."

She spat on her palm and rubbed the moisture over the tip, then, keeping the other end still tucked deep inside her body, she bent over me and nudged the tip against my lips.

"I should have eaten you," she whispered, bending to kiss me quickly. "I'm gonna come quick."

"I don't mind so long as you don't come off the cock. Keep fucking me until you're hot again."

With her hand guiding the dildo, she rocked her hips, stroking forward, pushing the head between my lips and entering me. I got my knees under me for leverage and leaned way back, meeting her strokes as her movements crammed it deeper and deeper inside me.

Watching the sway of her tits, the way they quivered at the end of a hard stroke, I wished I could take one of the tips into my mouth, but she'd have to rise up a bit first.

"Want it?" she said, cupping her breast, tweaking the tip and jiggling her breast to tempt me.

I swallowed hard, my pussy swelling, heating around the thrust of the dildo. I shook back my hair and met her gaze.

Who was the aggressor now? Ramona's smile was wide and wicked. She rose, letting the dildo slip partially out, and then aimed a breast at my mouth.

I rooted at it, teeth and lips clamping hard.

She gave a broken yelp then groaned, straining to slam down on the cock again, but I wouldn't let the little nipple go. I bit her, then soothed the ache with my tongue, all the while staying latched on the breast, suctioning hard enough that I felt a quiver rack her body.

"Fuck!" she groaned. "Cath...*Jesus*!"

I opened my mouth, releasing her.

She slammed down, then stroked forward hard, shoving the dildo into me and screwing her hips around and around so that its ridged girth stimulated every nerve ending deep inside me.

Suddenly, she leaned back, reaching down to smooth the kink I'd made at the center of the double-headed cock. Then we both pushed pillows under our shoulders, and stretched our legs alongside our bodies and shook and shimmied our hips, fucking in tandem, grinding together until we'd swallowed the whole length. Our pussies met in a moist hot kiss, her bristles scraping into my nude pussy.

At the last, I turned my head, scrunched my face and my mouth widened around a silent scream as the tight coil of my arousal exploded.

Fingers crept into the top of my folds, a soft pad swirling on my knot, sustaining the orgasm, making me jerk at the end and gasp because it was so strong, so tight that every muscle of my abdomen, belly and buttocks clenched hard.

She brought me down slowly, and I opened my eyes to find her sitting up, legs splayed around mine as she petted my belly and pussy.

I opened my mouth to say something, but I wasn't verbal yet. My mind was mush, my tongue thick. I think my ears were ringing, too. "What the fuck?" I finally rasped, cupping my own breasts for comfort as the tremors eased.

"Liked that, did you?" she said, sounding very pleased with herself.

"I think you fucking killed me."

She scooted back until the dildo fell from her pussy and pulled the other end out of me. Wrinkling her nose, she tossed it over the side of the bed and then crawled over me.

With my legs splayed, my body coated in a light sheen of

sweat, I must have looked like a well-used whore.

She didn't seem to mind, rubbing her belly and chest against me, and then lying over me like a blanket, her legs between mine. Her mouth rubbed the edge of my jaw, urging me to lift my chin. She licked my neck and slid down to kiss and lick my breasts.

I clutched the back of her head, forced her head up and came off the bed to kiss her hard. "We're doing this again."

"We have all night."

I shook my head. "No, dating again."

"This was a date?" she drawled.

"It's not just a hookup, dammit."

"You're right." She sighed and tucked her head against my shoulder. "It was...nice."

I held her, brushing her forehead with my mouth. She relaxed inside my embrace, and then a yawn eased her closer still.

She hadn't argued with me.

"But we're taking this slowly," she said, one last stubborn token of resistance.

I smiled. "Sure," I said, "as slow as you need," knowing full well that what we had was too hot, too addictive for us to pull back now.

The table was crowded after our shift. The pitcher of beer was nearly empty. Lonny stood at the counter flirting with a waitress. Ramona sat beside me. Jonesy sat next to her, grinning because he was the only one who could see her hand tucked between my thighs.

My face was flushed. Sweat beaded on my forehead. One more press of her fingers against the crotch of my pants, and I'd have to learn to walk with my legs crossed because I'd be soaked through.

"So, Cath," Jonesy drawled, "you seem to be settling in."

The bastard expected me to talk while Ramona's fingers strummed my pussy under the table.

Jonesy was her friend, and I knew now that they'd slept together when Ramona had first come to Canaan. They teased each other like sister and brother now.

I could use a little less familial love. I narrowed my eyes and clamped my thighs closed, trying to stop her play.

"Heard you were out at Schwieg's again," he said, his chest shaking because Ramona was pinching my pussy between two fingers, hard enough that I relented and eased my thighs open again.

"Yeah, can't believe he asked for me this time."

"You seem to have a real gift for pennin' pigs."

I shook my head, telling him silently that I was going to make him pay, but he only laughed, set down his glass and rose. "You two be good," he said, softly enough so only we could hear him before he called out farewells to the rest.

Ramona leaned in. "Give me five then I'll meet you at the door."

"Buck-fuckin'-naked, bitch."

Her laughter rang all the way to the door.

Lonny glanced over his shoulder, his gaze following Ramona as she left. Then he swung my way and strolled over to the table.

He sat in Ramona's vacated seat, careful not to move in too close. "You're all right, ya know."

I eyed him, meeting his steady stare. "I know that."

He shook his head. "I made a mistake, but you shouldn't blame me. You're a good-lookin' girl."

"Thank you, Lonny."

"If ever..."

I laid a hand on his thigh. "Don't spoil it," I warned him.

The corners of his mouth twitched. "Gonna take that Taser to me, Cath?"

Lonny wasn't such an idiot after all.

DRESS UNIFORM

Teresa Noelle Roberts

A re you kidding? I can't wear my uniform to the Fetish Fair!"
I smiled as I said it, though, because Lisette was wheedling
like a kid who wanted candy, and it was pretty damn adorable.
Lisette looks like an anime girl, all big eyes, big smile and big
breasts, and she was using all three of those attributes to good
effect. Usually when she makes her eyes wide, smiles eagerly and
poses so I can't help but look at her cleavage, I'll give in to just
about anything she wants, especially if she's also wearing a short
schoolgirl skirt or cat ears at the time.

This time I couldn't afford to give in. "I'd get in serious trouble
if the Chief found out. Besides, they'll have officers doing security detail. I don't want any confusion, especially if, god forbid,
there actually is a problem." Not that I expected problems. The
kink community may lead edgy sex lives, but we tend to be well-
behaved in public, if only to avoid anyone asking if dressing
your lover up in a pony harness violates some obscure local
ordinance. Whenever you get a few thousand people together,

though, there's a potential for weirdness—especially at a downtown convention center, where someone who thinks they're on a mission from god to get rid of pervs could pay their $20 and walk right in to cause trouble.

"How about your dress uniform? No one would get confused then."

I winced.

I'd just met Lisette the last time I had to haul out the dress uniform. I hadn't known the officer who'd been killed. He'd been from a different precinct, and we'd never run into each other on a detail or a Police Benevolent Association benefit. But that doesn't matter when one of your own buys it. You go to the funeral in your dress uniform, you're part of a strong wall of blue for the poor bastard's family and you hope you don't have to put on that uniform again for a long, long time—and that no one ever has to put it on for you until you die of old age.

Joe Morrissey had died less than four months ago. It was way too soon to put that uniform on for anything less than the President coming to our town and needing a police escort. Certainly not to gratify the whim of a lover. A uniform that still had a mass card in the pocket from a fellow officer's funeral wasn't sexy.

I didn't say a word, but I'm not as tough as I like to pretend I am, because my eyes got misty at the memory. Within a second, Lisette dropped her cutesy face and was holding me. "Sorry, Barb. I wasn't thinking. That was a bad idea."

I let her distract me with a kiss, because at that point I could use the distraction. As I'd hoped, Lisette's lips on mine and her curvy little body pressed up against me wiped away memories of a sea of blue in a packed church and a dead cop in his own dress uniform.

In fact, Lisette managed to wipe away all thoughts except

getting us both naked as quickly as possible. We didn't even bother heading for the bedroom, just took advantage of the big, comfy couch. She laid me down and kissed her way down my body, leaving smeary trails of red lipstick, until she was between my legs, half-sprawled off the couch.

She looked up at me and smiled like a mischievous little girl. Then she began to lick.

Lisette and I liked spanking and rope bondage and toys. I loved seeing her dressed up like the anime characters she resembles—and fucking her in those outfits. We're both a little addicted to leather. But sometimes it's good to get back to basics.

And there was nothing more basic than a beautiful woman licking your pussy.

Lisette's tongue teased my labia. She traced the outer lips until I was squirming and gasping. She then turned her attention to the inner ones, suckling first one then the other while taking care to just miss my clit.

My breath came in short gasps. My lower body rippled involuntarily. She ran her tongue down and up my slit, over and over again, lapping up my juices, which only flowed faster. I tangled my fingers in her short, wine-red hair and tugged. Her breath quickened at the small gesture of dominance, and that was what I wanted to hear. I could have moved her face then, directed her so she was focused on my clit, but that wasn't the point right now. The point was Lisette got hot from hair-pulling. Since the more sensitive parts of her were out of easy reach, I figured it was the least I could do.

She showed her appreciation by finally applying that talented tongue to my clit.

It wasn't the Fourth of July, but nevertheless fireworks exploded inside me. I shouted loudly enough that it might have scared the neighbors into calling the cops if I hadn't been one.

Naturally, once I regained motor coordination, I recipro-
cated.

Nothing like some spontaneous nookie to shake you out of
melancholy. By the time I'd licked the last drop of Lisette's juices
from my lips and we were cuddled together on the couch, idly
rummaging through the coffee-table stash of take-out menus
in search of dinner inspiration, I'd almost forgotten the whole
uniform conversation.

So of course Lisette had to bring it up.

She's stubborn and bratty like that sometimes. That's probably why we're good for each other. Her brattiness shakes me out
of my own head, which is where I'd otherwise end up stuck after
a long day of dealing with society's less charming elements.

But sometimes it was aggravating.

This was one of those times. When she said, "Okay, so I
understand about the uniform and the Fetish Fair. But how
come you'll never leave your uniform on when we fool around?
It would be so hot to be spanked by a cop," I lost it.

I made a habit of not blowing up at people I love. There's
a stereotype that either cops aren't there for loved ones at all
or they're grouchy bastards (and probably drunks) because of
stress and the knowledge that one of the occupational hazards
of your job is violent death. Unfortunately the stereotype has a
lot of truth behind it. Made me determined not to do the same.

So when I lost it, I did so in a very polite, controlled way.

I took a deep breath, counted to ten and then to twenty. Then
I added another ten for good measure before I actually spoke.

I still ended up snarling.

"I'm not a fetish, Lisette. My uniform isn't a cos-play outfit
or a vest and leather pants. Every time I've spanked you, you've
been spanked by a cop. By me. By a woman you say you care
about. And if that's not good enough for you, if you need the

fucking uniform, I don't know what to do, because I can't treat it like fetish gear."

Lisette's big eyes got even bigger. For a second I thought she might cry and it scared the hell out of me, because that meant either she was manipulating me or I was being a complete asshole despite my efforts to keep my anger under control. Neither option was good.

Then she looked away. "I have a uniform fetish," she muttered, so quietly I wasn't sure I heard her right.

"What?"

She repeated, more clearly this time, but still looking away, "I have a uniform fetish. It's why you caught my eye in the first place. You looked so strong and delicious in uniform that I just had to get to know you better. I couldn't help imagining you spanking me or doing a take-down scene or…well, anything, really…wearing that uniform. But you always take your uniform off as soon as you get home. I know I've never said it was a kink of mine in so many words, but I've asked about it before and you look at me like I've grown another head. I've always been willing to dress up for you because I know you like it. It gets frustrating."

She breathed in like she wanted to say more, but I cut her off. "I'm going out for a while. I need to think."

"Don't be angry."

I wanted to scream at her: *Don't be angry? You just told me we're together because you're kinky for my uniform.* Then I realized it wouldn't be fair, since my initial impressions of her had been equally shallow. I saw her then-pink hair and her nose ring and her funky, alternative look—goth meets anime girl meets old-school punk—and decided that she was insanely hot. But when she got a better job that meant she had to hide the nose ring and wear mainstream clothes and dye her hair a slightly more natural color, I hadn't complained.

Had I? All right, maybe a little, but I'd gotten over it quickly.

And if she'd told me up front that she was so into uniforms, like I'd told her about my fascination with little anime girls, we might have been able to work something out. Something that did not involve my working clothes.

"I'm not angry," I said. "All right, I'm angry, but I'm pretty sure I'm over-reacting. That's why I need to go out for a while. I'll be back, though."

My dramatic exit was spoiled by the need to put my clothes back on.

But maybe the pause was good. It forced me to think.

Instead of just storming randomly into the night, I got into the car and headed to a neighborhood where Lisette and I sometimes partied. I parked illegally and entered a narrow brownstone converted into a shop.

I came out half an hour later with a red and black shopping bag in my hand and laughed when I saw the ticket tucked under my windshield wiper. I should have known it would happen.

I considered ripping it up but thought better of it. I could pull the ticket from the system, but I needed all the good karma I could collect. After all, I had a dangerous job—and even more dangerous, a girlfriend who was probably wondering if she should go home, block my emails and delete my number from her phone.

To my amazement, she was still at the apartment when I returned. She'd put on a set of my old sweats and was half-asleep on the couch, jumping awake when I opened the door. "Barb," she said, scrambling to her feet, "I'm so glad you came back."

"Had to," I said, angling my body so she wouldn't see the

bag. "I live here. But seriously," I added as her pretty face fell, "I'm glad you're still here. I didn't want to leave things the way we did."

"Hug?"

I nodded and almost before I finished, her arms were around me. "I'm so sorry, Barb. What I tried to say earlier came out all wrong."

I hoped not all wrong, because I'd just made a very expensive impulse purchase based on what she'd said.

I dropped the bag behind the coatrack, where she might not see it right away, and returned the hug.

Damn, she felt right in my arms. Sure, we happened to fit each other's fantasy look, but a lot of relationships started based on nothing more substantial than having an eye for curvy African-American women or redheads or tanned blonde athletes or whatever. Just because we each had a fetish for what the other wore didn't mean we didn't connect on other levels. We'd work this out somehow.

And with any luck, the contents of the bag would help.

"I don't want you to think," Lisette said, "that I'm only seeing you because of the uniform. The hot woman in uniform caught my eye, but I figured out quickly I just plain like you. And I like that you got all excited about my thing for cosplay, but whenever I said you look great in uniform, you'd just say thanks and not get that I really think you look great in uniform. I thought maybe the Fetish Fair would help me start the conversation." She shrugged. "I'm sorry I pushed it."

I hugged her again. "I'm sorry I barked at you. It took me by surprise, even though I guess you've dropped plenty of hints, because uniform kink isn't on my radar. My grandfather was a cop. My dad and aunt are cops. I'm a cop and so is my brother. Uniforms are what you wear to work, like a suit or one of those stupid Burger King shirts. I can't play in my real uniform, because it represents my job. We haven't been together all that long, but you know I take my work seriously. Too seriously, maybe…"

Lisette nodded. "But I can see why. There are jobs you can leave at work, and then there are jobs where there's too much at stake. At least you're not totally wrapped up in a job whose only purpose is to make money for someone else. That would piss me off. Your job matters."

I thought about that dress uniform, about the last time I'd worn it. It must have showed on my face, because she added, "Life-or-death-level matters. I wouldn't expect a doctor to get hot and bothered by putting on her white coat and latex gloves, so I shouldn't expect it of you."

I thought for a minute. "But the doctor might like putting on a fake police uniform, or a nun's habit, or whatever, and a cop might like one of those crazy latex nurse uniforms."

Lisette laughed. "I hope that's not your secret fantasy! I mean, I'm willing to try anything once, but those don't do it for me."

I patted the sofa. "Wait here," I said. "I'll be right back."

I waved the bag teasingly at Lisette and headed into the bedroom.

Ten minutes later, I emerged in something that approximated my real-life uniform in the same way a short, shiny, latex Nurse Goodbody outfit approximated something you'd see at a doctor's office.

It was blue and gray. It had a generic badge in the right place. Unlike the faux nurse outfit, it covered most of the places a real uniform would, but, made of latex, it fit like a second skin and accented the breasts and butt that a real uniform downplayed. The "nightstick" would deliver a sweet thud on your favorite "criminal's" cute butt and could double as a dildo. I'd opted not to buy the cleverly molded but creepy gun-shaped dildo that was an option with the set. Only the polished black boots and black-leather search gloves were my own.

Well, and the handcuffs, but those were our fur-lined leather play cuffs, not the chintzy ones that came with the outfit and certainly not my real ones. Real cuffs hurt if you struggle, and Lisette likes to squirm.

I felt like a member of the Village People (only with cleavage) in the shiny, tight outfit, and my credit card was really, really annoyed with me.

But Lisette's face lit up. "Barb, that's...that's...oh, my god, thank you."

I might never understand her uniform fetish, but wearing a ridiculous outfit was a small price to pay for that look on her face, the wide, unfocused eyes and soft smile that told me, more surely than words, that she was getting wet.

"Strip," I ordered, brandishing my kinky nightstick. It didn't brandish well, being made of silicone rather than hard plastic, but it got the point across.

"You can't make me!" she exclaimed, gesturing melodramat-ically. "I want my lawyer!"

"Actually, I can make you." I did my best to sound menacing but started chuckling by the time I got to *can*. It didn't keep me from grabbing Lisette and ripping her clothes off—with her enthusiastic help.

I was still laughing when I pulled her down onto my vinyl-clad lap and cuffed her hands together behind her back.

Then I looked at her gleaming, slick pussy and her sweetly curved ass, straining up as she offered herself to me. I stopped laughing. I might feel like a complete fool in the outfit, but her reaction was worth it.

"It doesn't feel like your real uniform," she whispered. "It actually feels better."

"Polyester isn't very sexy. But what I'm wearing certainly is my uniform. I have the receipts to prove it." No point in role-playing, which was good because I could never keep it up for long.

And then I began to smack my lovely naked criminal with the faux nightstick in a way you're definitely not supposed to do in real life.

Though if you could, it would either reduce crime or encourage it.

Lisette let out a shocked gasp. She always does the first time, even if she knows exactly what's coming. Then she shuddered and whispered, "More, officer. It's got to be illegal the way I lust after this hot cop I know."

"Nothing illegal in knowing what you like." I punctuated the remark with a smack for each word, leaving delicious red marks on her fair skin.

But appropriate as the nightstick might be, it wasn't intimate enough.

My leather-clad hand was.

I brought it down on Lisette's hot ass again and again, making her writhe and cry out, beg for mercy and beg for more. Her heat poured into me through the leather glove and the vinyl clothing. She was flooding the leg of the pants with her smoky juices, and I was flooding the crotch—good thing the clerk at the store had thrown in some cleaner and maintenance instructions, because I was already sticky and we were just getting started.

With my free hand, I gripped her hair, pulling her head back hard so I could see her face. It was mottled, and she looked like she might have been crying, but she wore a blissed-out smile. I took a second's break to kiss her. The angle meant it was short and superficial, but it still jolted me even higher.

"Beautiful," I murmured. Then I let her lower her head.

And picked up the dildo.

Lisette raised her hips to give me better access, and her molten pussy welcomed the penetration. It took me a few strokes to get the rhythm down, but soon I got it. Smack. Fuck. Smack. Fuck. As I watched the beautiful girl going crazy across my lap, I couldn't help thinking that this moment belonged in an adult version of one of those credit card commercials. "Fetish outfit: $300. Sex toy: $75. Incredibly aroused woman moaning and writhing on your lap: priceless."

I even considered sharing the thought with her. We often joked around in bed, and it was a funny image.

But Lisette started to come, and all thought left me except how wonderful it was to watch orgasm overtake her, to know I'd caused it.

Well, me and a pervy fashion designer and the nice guy at the fetish store who'd helped me pick out just the right outfit. But I was willing to take the credit.

Lisette came more than I'd ever seen her come—and she was always multi-orgasmic, so that was saying something. When she finally collapsed limp and spent across my knees, I uncuffed her and snuggled her on my lap, her head leaning against the plastic badge. "Thank you," she whispered, her voice hoarse from screaming. "That may be even better than the real deal. Uniform fetish meets cosplay."

"Lucky guess. Okay, not just luck. I know you like how latex feels, and I know I like how it looks on you, so it seemed like a plan."

"Do you get the uniform thing any better now?"

"I get that you really, really like it, and that's what matters. I can't imagine ever wanting to play in my real uniform—but I can in this, because it's made to be sexy. And if this is a compromise you can live with, I'll be glad to dress up for you. Just not as a real police officer."

She nodded. "Your real uniforms are special. Serious. I can understand why you don't want to play in them. But it'll always make me hot to see you dressed for work. Hot and proud."

Once she said that, I couldn't resist kissing her.

Which just got us started again—this time with a cat-girl teasing a poor, hapless cop.

A COP'S WIFE

Evan Mora

There's an empty wine bottle on the kitchen counter and an empty glass beside it. Good thing it was half empty when I began, otherwise I might really be in trouble.

Half empty.

There was a time when I was a half full kind of girl. I could find a silver lining in any cloud.

"Always so damned optimistic," Patrice would laugh, shaking her head with amusement.

"One of us has to be!" I'd jokingly reply. Such was the yin and yang of our relationship: I did feel-good humanitarian pieces for the city paper, and Patrice was a Detective with the Sex Crimes Unit. We had a good balance, and it had served us well in our life together—at least it had until I picked up the phone one otherwise unremarkable evening and our world changed.

"Is this Amie?"

"Yes, it's Amie."

"Amie Norris?"

"That's right."

"The wife of Detective Sergeant Patrice LaMarque?"

"Yes..." I'd been hesitant by then. He'd spoken quietly, but there'd been something in his tone that didn't sit right with me.

"Can I help you?" I'd asked briskly.

"Yes. You can help me, Amie; you can deliver a message for me. You can tell Detective LaMarque that I know her license plate number, and I know your home address. And you can tell her that I'm going to kill her."

Patrice was fierce. Phone records were pulled, patrol cars swept our sleepy residential neighborhood every half hour, wiretaps on our phones—everything that could be done was done.

"What can you tell me about his voice?" Patrice's steely gray eyes bored into mine.

"I...I don't really know."

"Did he speak with any discernable accent?"

"Not that I recall..."

"Did he sound old? Young?"

"Patrice..." I shrugged miserably.

"*Merde*!" She bit off the curse, exhaling heavily and running an impatient hand through her close-cropped dark hair. Tears pooled helplessly in my eyes. Seeing them, Patrice dropped to her knees in front of my chair, framed my face with her hands and forced me to meet her eyes.

"I'm sorry, *chère*, please don't cry," she said gently.

"I'm scared, Patrice—what do I do if something happens to you? And the kids! He said he knows where we live. What if—"

Patrice's kiss cut off the flow of my words, her mouth moving over mine with the sureness and familiarity of a decade of togetherness; of a life built on love and passion and trust. I kissed her with all the fear and desperation I felt, and she took it, eased it, gave me a measure of calm. When it ended, she pressed her forehead against mine as I took a steadying breath.

"Amie, I need you to be strong," she said. "You are the sun that holds us all in orbit—me, the kids—you are the center of our universe. This man is a coward, nothing more, and nothing is going to happen to me. Do you understand? Nothing."

I nodded my head, squared my shoulders. "You're right." I said it with a conviction I didn't quite feel and a weak smile that I'm sure didn't reach my eyes, determined, for her sake, to show a brave face. Keep Calm and Carry On, as the saying goes.

Being a cop's wife is a particular life. There is an understanding that, on any given day, the likelihood that bad things could happen to your spouse is much greater than if they were, say, an accountant, or a school teacher. You imagine what it would feel like to get the phone call, or the knock on the door, that tells you that they've been injured, or worse, that they've been killed.

People say, "I don't know how you do it," but the fact of the matter is, that despite this understanding, the fear remains mostly abstract because by and large, nothing does happen. And at the end of the day, you trust in the training and the instincts and the support that enable these men and women to do their jobs and protect the public.

Patrice had been in tight scrapes before and had always emerged unscathed. And this wasn't an irate, abusive husband pointing a gun at her chest, or a rapist she'd just chased into a dark, dead-end alley. It was just a threat. Just an anonymous voice on the phone.

A week went by. A week that, but for the patrol cars silently passing our block, looked like any other week. We ate breakfast together, Patrice kissed the kids good-bye on her way out the door, and I walked them to school and went to work. Our evenings were a jumble of swimming lessons and Little League and homework and the usual chaos that comes with raising two kids. It wasn't unusual for Patrice to miss dinner, and there were nights where she'd come home to tuck Jake and Ella into bed, read them a story and then leave again.

"You gotta catch the bad guys, right, *Maman*?" Jake would ask seriously, a frown creasing his seven-year-old brow.

"Right, *mon fils*, catch them and lock them up tight."

"Do the bad guys not go to sleep at night?" Ella, at five, had less of an understanding of the dangers the bad guys posed.

"No, *ma petite*, sometimes they don't." She'd smile, tousling Ella's long dark curls.

Patrice worked late every night that week, poring over case files past and current, trying to put a name to the voice on the phone. It would be midnight or later by the time she'd finally come home and fall exhausted into bed with me. And even then, I could feel the tension in her shoulders and see it in the set of her mouth. He was getting to her—whoever he was—and her frustration was palpable.

"He could be any one of a hundred men, Amie. How am I supposed to find him?"

"Shhh..." I brushed a gentle kiss across her lips and placed another on each of the deep lines that bracketed her mouth, lines born of laughter and worry both. I loved those lines; they spoke of hard work and good times and a wealth of experience that added to, rather than detracted from, the attractiveness of her face.

"Nothing's going to happen, remember?"

"I know, it's just—" I kissed her fully then, silencing her words and pressing my body against hers, offering her the comfort I knew she needed. Patrice groaned, her strong arms closing around me, holding me tight as she pressed me into the bed. Her thigh slid between mine; her hand sought out my heat as her body rocked against me.

"Amie!" She cried brokenly when she found release, her face buried in my neck as her body trembled.

"It's okay, baby," I murmured, running my fingers through the damp tendrils at the nape of her neck, kissing the shell of her ear. "It's okay" I repeated, whispering it again and again in the darkness, though secretly, I wasn't sure I believed it.

The nightmares started soon after that. She didn't tell me right away, but I didn't need to be a detective to figure out that she wasn't sleeping. Her restless tossing and turning and the dark circles under her eyes told me that.

"Patrice, you've got to get some rest." I watched her stumble toward the shower after yet another sleepless night. "Maybe we can get you something to help you sleep."

"No!" she snapped. Then more quietly, "No. I just...I don't..." she sighed heavily, looking at me with haunted eyes. "Every time I fall asleep I dream about him. I dream that he's here. That there's this faceless man standing over the bed with a gun pointed at my head. I feel...helpless. Stupid." She turned away from me, braced her arms on the vanity, her head hung low.

The confession cost her, I knew. Patrice, who was always so strong, who was always my safe haven in any storm, needed my strength now, needed me to be big while she felt small. I wrapped my arms around her waist and pressed my cheek against her shoulder.

"Not stupid, my love. Not at all. And there's nothing shameful about feeling fear. I'd be more worried if you weren't frightened."

Patrice laughed bitterly. "I'm a cop, Amie. I deal with things every day that most people don't see in a lifetime."

"Yes. And that's your job." I spun her around. "And you're very good at it. But that isn't personal and this is. This isn't some pedophile you're tracking down, Patrice; this man is threatening you. He's threatening us. Our life. Our family. Being afraid doesn't make you a coward, it makes you human."

"I know…"

"And I know what an amazing, strong woman you are and what an amazing detective you are. And I know that there is no one I trust more than you to keep us safe." She nodded her head, shaking off her mood.

"I'm going to get this bastard, Amie." The steel was back in her eyes, and I sent up silent thanks.

A week turned into two without any additional contact from the man on the phone. Patrol cars continued to drive by our house once or twice a night, but the growing hope was that this had been an idle threat, the cowardly prank of someone who had brushed with Patrice and come out on the losing end. But while I was cautiously optimistic that it was over and done with, Patrice was still edgy. I worried that she was holding on to this for the wrong reasons, that she felt compelled to keep searching because this man had somehow breached her defenses and made her feel weak, but she was steadfast in her belief that it wasn't over.

"It was too personal to be a prank." She picked up the thread of conversation once more, late into the evening when I was all but asleep, lulled by the sound of her heart beneath my cheek and the warm strength of her arm across my back.

"Oh, Patrice…" I murmured my protest against her skin, burrowed closer as though I could will myself back into that fleeting moment of peace.

"I know, *chère*, but he took the time to find our address, my license plate number, our home phone number. He knew your name—knew that you were my wife. If this had been an impulsive prank, he would have called the station and delivered his threat to the operator, or whoever had answered the phone at my desk. It's too calculated. I don't like it."

"Baby, please...just try to sleep?" I pleaded.

"Okay, okay," she groused half-heartedly, kissing the top of my head gently and turning out the light, "but I'd still feel more comfortable if I had my gun beneath my pillow."

I didn't answer other than to grunt at her; I didn't need to. Her gun was in the lockbox she kept on a shelf in her closet, where it was every night when she returned home. I didn't doubt that she'd feel more comfortable with her weapon close at hand, but it wasn't a risk you took with kids in the house.

As each day passed without incident, I felt as though things were returning to normal. Good things still happened in the world—I wrote about them every day. The kids, who had remained largely oblivious to the tension in the house, played happily with the other kids on the street.

I'd watered the plants on the front porch and was thumbing through the usual assortment of bills and junk mail that filled our mailbox when a large manila envelope with Patrice's name on the front caught my eye. I opened it and found a single photograph inside: a picture of the kids and me in the schoolyard, and on the back:

What a beautiful family you have, Detective LaMarque. It's a pity your children will grow up without you. I hope your pretty wife will be able to find someone to comfort her when you're gone.

The photograph slipped from my frozen fingers and for a moment I couldn't move, could barely breathe for the terror flooding through me. He had followed us. He had been here, on our front porch. He could be somewhere close by right now, watching us. My world became sharp and flat all at once: the street, all the houses, even the trees went gray; the sounds of the city all faded to dull insignificance. But the kids—suddenly everything around them seemed oversaturated with color, their clothes, their bicycles...their innocent laughter seemed like the only sound I could hear.

"Jake! Ella!" I ran down the steps and the few meters to where they were playing. "Inside. Now!"

"But, Mommy!" they chorused.

"No buts. Now!" I rushed them into the house, locked the door behind me and swiped at the tears that filled my eyes, aware that they didn't understand what was going on, and that I was scaring them too.

I punched Patrice's cell number into the phone with trembling fingers, cursing myself for not trusting her instincts and cursing the naïve optimism that had made me believe this was over.

There were no fingerprints on the photograph or the envelope, and it appeared doubtful that there'd be any DNA evidence either. The handwritten note had been sent off for analysis, but any clues it might yield would not be forthcoming this night. The patrol cars were back on their twice-hourly sweeps; other than that, there was nothing more that could be done.

In the early hours of morning, it was Patrice and I once more, alone in the dark. I'd convinced her to lie down with me, if only for the few hours that remained until dawn. I knew she wouldn't sleep. I wouldn't either for that matter, but I needed her close. I needed the reassurance of her skin against mine, and whether or not she'd admit it, she needed it too.

But even like this, held tight in the circle of her arms in the privacy of our bedroom, he was there. He was everywhere. His taint was like a mist curling in through a crack in the window, seeping under the doorframe, spilling through the keyhole. It was insidious, filling the inside of the room until I felt like I couldn't breathe again, until I felt like I was suffocating in fear and anger and despair.

Patrice was vibrating, struggling with emotions of her own. I knew I should say something about how everything would be okay, how I knew she would catch this filthy coward, but the words couldn't make it past the lump in my throat. I was determined not to cry—she didn't need that from me right now—but when she said, "I put a copy of my will in the lockbox," the tears fell of their own volition; she rocked me in the dark and nothing more was said.

It was 6:54 p.m. when she got the call. We were finishing dinner. She'd made a point to be there to share this time with the kids and me the past couple of days, though if I thought too much about her motivation, I was afraid I'd cry all over again. She picked up on the first ring, striding out of earshot and returning a few moments later, already sliding an arm into her navy blazer, drawing it up to cover the shoulder holster that carried her weapon.

"I've got to go," she told me tersely, barely breaking stride as she headed toward the door. I caught her as she drew it open.

"Patrice!" I laid a hand on her arm, stopping her progress, taking in her murderous look. "Tell me, please!" I begged.

"Call came in a few minutes ago," she said, barely-simmering rage in her voice. "Guy's holding his ex-wife and kids at gunpoint, refuses to talk to anyone but me."

"Is it?"

"It's him. Bastard just got paroled a couple of months ago. I remember this guy. We investigated allegations of sexual abuse called in by the school board a couple of years ago. This guy was molesting his two little girls—Amie, they weren't any older than Jake and Ella. Wife wouldn't talk; he was using her as a punching bag when he wasn't hurting his kids. The things he was doing to them... I'm sorry, *chère*, but I've got to go."

"Patrice..." She looked at me, waiting for me to say something. I wanted to tell her not to go, that she was walking into a trap, that this was exactly what this sicko wanted. I wanted to tell her I needed her too much to lose her, that the kids needed her too much to lose her. But I couldn't. Because this was what she did, who she was. And because somewhere in the city, there was another terrified woman with her two children who needed her even more than I did.

"Be safe." It was all I could manage. I stroked her cheek tenderly, trying to memorize her face as it looked in this moment, so afraid that I might lose her, knowing that I couldn't love her any more than I did right now. And then she was gone.

I poured myself a glass of wine, went about the business of getting the kids bathed and into bed, cleaned up the kitchen, straightened up the living room. I did all these things on autopilot, while in my head a mantra ran: *Please let her be okay, please let her be okay...* Then I ran out of things to do, so I just stood there at the kitchen counter, waiting.

A second glass of wine.

An empty bottle on the counter, and soon enough, my empty glass beside it.

A thousand what-ifs were all clamoring for attention on the periphery of my mind, but I couldn't entertain them. I couldn't allow them in. I couldn't allow any thought other than, please let her be okay.

And then the phone rang.

"Patrice?" I cried into the receiver. Oh, god, please let her—

"It's me, *chère*, I'm okay. It's over."

"Can you come home?" I needed to touch her, to know she was really safe.

"Soon, *chère*, I'll be home soon."

I was waiting outside, sitting on the porch step when she arrived. Part of me wanted to hurl myself into her arms and give in to the great wracking sobs that I was holding onto by a thread. But the greater part of me needed more than the simple release crying would provide.

"Amie?" Her voice was little more than a whisper of sound in the quiet of the night.

I stood up on the step and opened my arms to her, closed my eyes against the almost painful relief that surged through my body at the feel of her pressed against me. Patrice stroked my back, my arms, anywhere she could reach, her mouth seeking out mine with an urgency that matched my own.

"You're okay," I murmured against her lips. I traced the contours of her face with my fingertips, then her eyebrows, her cheekbones, her beautiful square jaw, placing reverent kisses everywhere I touched, feeling the shudder that traveled through her body.

"Mmmm..." She captured my lips again, slanted her mouth aggressively across mine, bruised my lips with the force of her kiss and pulled me more tightly against her. "Amie, I need you so bad right now. I'll tell you everything later, I promise, but for now can we—"

I let my kiss answer her unspoken question. I knew how she felt. After all these weeks of vacillating between belief and disbelief, strength and weakness, between calm assurances and horrible despair, I needed her, the indisputable, solid proof that she was real, beneath my hands, against my flesh, more than I needed air to breathe.

Once upstairs I turned on the bedside lamp, disrobed and slid between the sheets while Patrice dealt with her service revolver and clothes. And then she was beside me and nothing else—not the horrible things that had happened this night or whatever was to come tomorrow—mattered. I shivered when she stroked my neck, when her fingers trailed across my collarbone and down over the swell of my breast, tracing my contours, circling my nipple and teasing it to hardness.

"You know what I kept thinking?" She frowned, leaning in to press a kiss between my breasts. "That it couldn't be my time, because I haven't loved you enough yet."

"Oh, Patrice," I murmured, framing her face with my hands and drawing her up to look in my eyes, "there's no such thing as *enough*." I kissed her tiny frown lines. "I will spend the rest of my life loving you, and it still won't be enough."

She kissed me with a groan, sliding her tongue into my mouth as she moved, settling her hips between my legs, bracing herself on her forearms above me. I loved the weight of her, the heat of our bodies pressed together, the sublime feel of her breasts crushed against mine. I wanted to spend all night loving her, slowly and thoroughly, but the feel of her fevered skin on mine was sending me up in flames, all the anguish and desperation I'd felt when she'd left earlier burning away like so many logs on the fire. My restless hands roamed her back and lower, skimmed across her ass, pulled her deeper into the cradle of my hips.

Patrice's mouth blazed a trail from my mouth to my neck and down to my breasts, drew first one and then the other into the warm heat of her mouth, lavished each with equal attention. I moaned my pleasure, delved my hands into her rich dark hair, pressed her closer still. Her teeth grazed the aching peak of one nipple while she teased the other into rigidity between her thumb and forefinger.

"Patrice, I...please..." I didn't know what I was asking for, but it wasn't enough, I needed more. Patrice bit down on the nipple held captive in her mouth and pinched the other until I gasped, then eased the tiny hurts with a soft stroke of her tongue before moving lower, trailing open-mouthed kisses down my belly, across my hip, over the soft skin of my inner thigh.

She stroked the heat that greeted her, teasing the moisture there before retreating, spreading my lips apart to reveal flesh swollen with need. She inhaled my arousal, tasted it, ran her tongue along my length before moving forward to tease my clit. A tremor took hold deep inside me, and my fingers crept back into her hair.

"Oh, yes, baby..." I breathed, and Patrice groaned in response, no teasing now, her own need rising as she buried her face in my folds, feasting on the arousal that met her, thrusting her tongue into my wetness, devouring me with a hunger equal to my own. She turned her attention to my clit, circling the hardness with her tongue and nipping the sensitive tissue before settling into a rhythm, urged on by the pressure of my hands on her head and the increasing volume of my moans. I rode the waves of pleasure with Patrice my only anchor, my world reduced to her mouth and the divine feel of her tongue. But still I needed more, my muscles tensing and my grip on Patrice tightening as tension coiled in my belly.

"Please, Patrice..." I begged, "I need you inside me..." I needed so much more than that. I needed her buried so deeply that I could never lose her; that she would become an indelible part of me, burned into my flesh.

"I'm here, *chère*," she whispered, stealing my next breath with her kiss, one leg sliding over mine while her hand trailed down my abdomen. Her fingers brushed through my damp curls, and then she was thrusting into me, filling my emptiness, easing the ache inside me as only she could. I could feel her slick arousal on my thigh, her hips rocking against me in time with her thrusts, driven by the need that consumed her.

"Yes, baby...that's it." I urged her on, pushed my hips upward, forced her to the edge. Patrice moaned, her clit crushed against me, thrusting into me and against me with a passion that bordered on violence until we both cried out, rocked by the intensity of the release that crashed over us, clinging to each other until the tremors subsided.

I stroked her hair tenderly. We had weathered this storm. And no matter what lay ahead, I knew we would prevail over any uncertainty.

"Are you okay?" I asked, searching her eyes for the truth.

"How could I be otherwise?" She smiled tenderly. "I'm with you—my wife, my sun, the center of my universe."

CHARITY AND SPLENDOR

Andrea Dale

I was elbow deep in soapy dishwater when my eleven-year-old daughter Ashley came into the kitchen, her blue eyes brimming with unshed tears.

"What's wrong, honey?" I grabbed a cobalt-and-white striped dishtowel to dry my hands.

"Mom," she said, "it's about the dogs."

I sighed. She'd wanted a dog for a while, but between her school and activities, and my work, we didn't have enough time for one.

Before I could say anything, she went on. "The police dogs. They don't have enough money for bulletproof vests for them, and one of them got shot recently."

"Oh, honey." I pulled her in close. Ashley had a bleeding heart when it came to animals; I knew this was killing her. Her voice muffled, she went on to tell me that the K-9 dog had, in fact, survived surgery, but wasn't there anything we could do?

"We could donate some money," I offered. The coffers were

tight, but not so much that we couldn't occasionally give a little. It was something I'd tried to instill in Ashley, like donating the toys she no longer played with to a women's shelter.

"It's not enough," she said, pulling away from me, her voice now as strident and fierce as a preteen's could be. The tears lingered on her lashes, but they framed eyes filled with resolve. "The vests are seriously expensive—way too much for just us. Can we do a fund-raiser or something? Get lots of people involved?"

Kids. They'll break your heart with their wonderfulness.

We enlisted the help of her teacher, Mr. Schindling, and the other dog-crazy girls in her class. The girls brainstormed ways to make money, came up with a logo, brought the enthusiasm. I agreed to handle the aspects the girls couldn't: opening a PayPal account, for example, and sending a press release to the local paper.

But all that was after I called the police department and set up an appointment for Ashley and me to meet with the head of the K-9 unit.

"Rosa Mendez," she said, holding out her hand.

"Monica Westberg."

We shook briefly, and then she led us to a small office.

She had that cop demeanor, not quite militaristic, but still with squared shoulders, a no-nonsense expression and clipped speech. It's not that she was unfriendly—hey, even the cops that had pulled me over once (okay, maybe twice) for speeding had been polite when they'd handed me my ticket—but she was businesslike to the extreme. Just a quick smile for Ashley.

Everything changed, though, when I let Ashley explain why we were there.

It was the smile that did me in. The astonished grin that blossomed across her face, the dimple on the left side, the flash of light in her dark eyes. "Are you *serious*?" she said.

"Absolutely," I said. "Of course, we won't do anything without the full support of the department."

"We'd be insane not to," Rosa said. "Ashley, you are an extraordinary young woman."

Ashley blushed and ducked her head, and I liked Rosa even more.

We talked about getting some information and materials from her about the K-9 program, and then Rosa asked if we'd like to meet Duke, the dog who'd been shot.

I thought Ashley was going to vibrate out of her anime hoodie at the very prospect.

Duke was hanging out with the other dogs who weren't out on patrol with their handlers, although Duke had a private enclosure since he was recovering. His tail started wagging as soon as he saw Rosa, and if she'd had a tail, it would've wagged, too.

She talked about Duke with deep affection, and I heard her voice quaver once before she cleared her throat and mentioned the surgery he'd gone through. She kept the details fuzzy for Ashley's sake.

And all the while I was thinking, dammit, I have the worst timing when it comes to crushes.

Well, this was going to be awkward.

The first time Rosa came to the house with materials for Pause for the Paws Cause, I was ridiculously nervous. I didn't have time to both deep clean the house and go all out primping myself, and for the first time in ages, I chose myself. The house wasn't in bad shape, or so I told myself as an excuse.

Finally I settled on a way-too-expensive pair of jeans I'd splurged on (because they really did hide a multitude of flaws) and a purple sweater that showed a little cleavage.

I wanted to believe Rosa had been thinking along the same lines. She wore a flowered top, all muted mauves and washed-silk greens, and a green, flowing, silk skirt that flipped out at the ends just about the knee. I guess, having only seen her in uniform, I hadn't expected that. Now all I could wonder is whether, under her uniform and right now, she wore delicate lacy underthings.

Yes, boys, even girls think that way.

Rosa complimented me on the house and moved around the living room to look at the family photos. Most were of Ashley and me, but I did have one out with Jane.

"So," she said finally, "I take it there's no Mr. Westberg?"

"There never was," I said. "My partner and I chose to have Ashley—I carried her—but Jane died when Ashley was two. Ashley doesn't really remember her."

I wanted to watch Rosa's face when I said it, to see her reaction, but I also didn't want to. I was reasonably confident I wouldn't see a negative reaction, but I didn't want to see politeness, distance, or pity.

When I was in my twenties, it was easier to find a like-minded woman. There were bars, clubs, friends-of-friends. Now, in my early forties, I had a daughter and a career, and no time for a wild nightlife. I had friends, but they didn't have many single friends. And I was picky about who I'd let get close because of Ashley.

Not that I was overthinking any of this, of course.

"I'm sorry about your partner," Rosa said, her voice soft. "That must have been very hard."

"We had some wonderful times together," I said. "And I'm glad for Ashley. I might not have gotten pregnant if Jane and I hadn't been together."

"She's an amazing girl," Rosa agreed, and again I liked what the warm smile did to her face, to her big brown eyes. "You've done a great job with her."

"Sometimes I think I've just been lucky," I said.

Rosa shook her head, serious again. "No," she said. "I've seen all types of people, Monica, and sure, occasionally someone can dig their way out of a bad family. But almost always, it's the support of the parents that influences how kids turn out."

"Well, then, thank you," I said, just in time for Ashley to come bounding into the room, burbling with questions about how Duke was doing.

We worked closely together over the next couple of months—oh, sure, with Ashley and Mr. Schindling and the rest of the girls. But I was certain it wasn't my imagination that Rosa found excuses to call or stop by, hand-delivering photos for the website instead of emailing them to me.

I wasn't above texting her to update her on a new donation or fund-raising idea, either.

Were we flirting? I thought so. I hoped so. It had just been a long time since I'd engaged in any sort of courtship behavior, and so often Ashley was around...

Then one night Ashley was staying over at a friend's, and Rosa brought Duke (who curled up on a corner and didn't knock anything over like he had last time), take-out and a bottle of wine. We filled our plates with Chinese and curled up on the sofa across from each other. She preferred a fork, and I appreciated it, having never been adept with chopsticks myself. We joked about that, chatted about our day, about nothing and everything.

Once we'd finished, we drew chairs up to the computer so we could go over the latest flyer before it was printed. I opened the email account we'd set up for the fund-raising project, and gasped.

"What is it?" she asked, leaning so close I could smell her shampoo, something clean and fresh.

I pointed at the message from a local engineering firm. "Mes-

Tech says they'll match all non-business donations! That'll more than double what we've brought in!"

The community had already come out to support Pause for the Paws Cause, and we'd made a nice chunk of change. The funds matching brought it into the realm of hot-damn amazing.

Rosa shrieked with joy, throwing her arms around me. I returned the hug, thrilled both by the news and by the feel of her arms around me.

That's when everything shifted. One moment a friendly celebratory hug, and the next we both seemed to realize simultaneously how close our faces were to each other. I couldn't say, then or later, who kissed who first. There was a mutual hesitation, and then we both decided the same thing at the same time.

She tasted like chablis, and her lips were soft against mine. We were tentative, exploring, and that was fine. It wasn't about passion, not yet. It was about introduction and discovery.

We both leaned back, stared at each other and started talking at once.

"I hope that was okay—"

"I wasn't sure if you—"

We laughed. "You first," she said.

I took a deep breath. Where to begin? I felt like a fumbling teenager again, giddy and terrified and awkward in equal measure.

"I haven't done this in a while," I said.

"From my end, I can say you were doing *just* fine," she said in a purr that started a slow, delicious heat roiling in my belly.

"I meant dating," I said. "But yeah, it's been a while for that, too."

Her arm was still around me; she gently stroked my back. "I understand," she said. "No pressure."

We'd already talked about how I wasn't going to bring

anybody home until I was sure where things were going, because that wasn't fair to Ashley.

"Well," I said, "on the plus side, Ashley already knows you and likes you."

"I like her, too," Rosa said. "But right now, I'm liking you a lot more."

If it didn't work out with Rosa, I rationalized, it wouldn't be a huge hiccup in our family life. We had only a month left on the fund-raising campaign; she'd have eased out of lives by then anyway.

I suppose in other circumstances we'd have taken it slow. But we'd already been taking it slow, dancing around our mutual desire for so long I thought I was going to lose my mind. To find out it *was* mutual had tripped a switch in my brain.

"Good thing," I said. "Because she won't be home 'til tomorrow afternoon, so I'm all you've got."

Rosa did, I discovered to my delight, indeed have a penchant for skimpy, lacy underthings. When I confessed my fantasies about that, she chuckled.

"Ever since I met you, I've gotten dressed each day wondering whether you'd like this set or that one," she said.

"So far, I approve," I said.

The demi-cup bra cradled her small, round breasts, the cherry-red color a perfect shade against her dusky skin. The matching panties had faux lacing up the front, the ribbon tied in a jaunty bow. I'd get to that.

For now I fastened my mouth onto the nipple that pressed insistently against her bra and suckled her through the lace. She arched her back, murmuring something in Spanish. I didn't know what it was, but it sounded incredibly seductive. I pushed the lace aside, wanting to feel and taste her flesh, wanting to hear her murmurs and cries and moans.

I grazed her collarbone with my teeth, worked my way down her body. She was strong from her regular workouts but soft in all the right places. I tugged at the ribbon on her panties with my teeth, too, making her laugh and squirm.

Her panties were already damp, and I breathed in the spicy scent of her. "Monica," she whispered, her hands moving restlessly on the sheets.

I eased the panties down her legs, darted my tongue into her folds. It had been a long time, yes, but I hadn't forgotten the joy of urging another woman to orgasm: the joy of discovering what she liked, what made her cry out, what made her come.

Rosa squirmed, tensed, sobbed out my name as she pulsed and clenched around my fingers deep inside her, and a tiny tremor echoed in my own pussy.

Then she was sliding down, urging me onto my back, kissing her juices on my lips as I ground my crotch into her knee, then following a similar path down my body to the one I'd taken down hers. It might have been my turn to cry out her name, but I'm never that coherent. I whispered it afterwards, into her hair, as we cuddled.

I thought about getting up and retrieving the wine bottle and glasses, but when I rolled over, I discovered Duke in the bedroom doorway, his head cocked as he regarded us.

"That's...disconcerting," I said.

"You get used to it," Rosa said, and proceeded to distract me.

Even after Pause for the Paws Cause wrapped, we kept seeing each other, and we talked about a lot of things. The danger her job put her in and the sometimes strange hours. The difficulty of integrating a new person into a family unit. The fact that she was seven years younger than me.

In the end, though, there was no question how we felt about each other and what we wanted for the future.

We sat Ashley down at the kitchen table. My mouth was dry. How would she handle this? What if she didn't come to love Rosa the way I did?

I carefully told her that Rosa and I had been seeing each other.

"Oh, *Mom*," Ashley said. "I know that already. It's *obvious*."

Rosa and I exchanged startled glances as I replayed the past year in my head, trying to figure out where we'd slipped.

"It is?" I asked, befuddled. "How?"

She rolled her eyes. "The very first time Rosa came over, you wore perfume. So, is Rosa going to move in? And does this mean we can have a dog?"

Kids. They'll keep you on your toes. I was going to be in so much trouble when Ashley hit her teens.

Rosa's hand crept into mine. The best part was, I wasn't going to have to go it alone anymore.

CHAPEL STREET BLUE

R. V. Raiment

With a long, drawn out "o-h-h" of weariness, Sally lies back in the bed. A familiar sound. A precious sound. I study her face and wait for her to talk.

"'You wouldn't mind taking hold of my nightstick, now would you, Sal?'"

She's quoting one of Loomis's jokes. He's her partner. Six foot two of beefcake, a lantern-jawed cliché and a jock, who'll tell you he went from tackling on the football field to tackling crime instead.

She's told me all about Todd Loomis, and often. Listening has become my role. Part of it, anyway.

"He never was particularly good at it, you know?" I do know, and I know it's football she's referring to, but my expression's noncommittal so she won't feel guilty for telling me all over again. "Never was really interested in anything but cheerleaders and groupies. Always looking for something half-undressed to 'twirl his baton.'"

She doesn't even react to his clumsy innuendoes anymore, she tells me. She just smiles that little smile which enables both of them to pretend that he's only pretending, that he doesn't *really* want to fuck her, that he doesn't long for the day when the tenor of that small smile changes and gives him permission to jump her bones.

That's what he wants. That's what they all want—all those not too old or addled, anyway. And why wouldn't they? Even Sally understands that. One look in a mirror and she understands that.

You can usually tell the gender of a cop at a glance. The blues, the holster on the utility belt, the leather jacket, they're power dressing with a vengeance, but it's actually very rare that you'll confuse a male cop with a female.

No one makes that mistake with Sally. No one could make that mistake with Sally. You see Sally in uniform on the street, and you look around for the HBO camera truck, the caterers and the focus pullers. Sally's got the face of a movie star and the body to go with it: breasts that beg similes of ripe fruit; an ass no one could compare to anything but peaches; long, long legs, reaching up to a heaven that every guy on the force would die to get into.

When she's in uniform, guys whistle. They try to hide it, of course. They try to duck their heads so that she won't know who it was who whistled, because while she's a stunner, there's something about Sally in uniform that's quite scary for most men. There's an indefinable power to her. One look and you know you'd never out-run her if she took exception and that it would take one helluva guy to overpower her. Like Todd, she's an athlete. Unlike Todd, she hasn't let recent years take the edge off her body.

In civvies… Well, she tries not to let the guys see her in civvies. She likes to give the impression she lives in her uniform, neat and clean and sharp as it always is, and hardly anyone has ever seen her out of it. She sunbathes on the flat roof of the brown-stone we live in, locking the access door behind us with a key she prised out of the janitor's keeping. And when she does go out sans uniform, hardly anyone would be able to tell you it was her. She finds baggy tracksuits and dark lenses useful that way, though the tracksuit that can truly camouflage that ass is rare.

Locking the roof access so she can sunbathe naked unob-served is, too, a kindness. Most of the men in our building are middle-aged and older. The sight of that body unadorned is, for most of them, potential heart-attack country.

She knows it, and it's part of what makes her different and makes her so very good at what she does.

The world is full of beautiful women who are quite unsur-prised at the scarcity of decent guys who want to be with them. Indecent or un-decent men who want to fuck them are a different matter. Such men are never, ever in short supply. But the lack of a White Knight is no surprise to your average Not-Quite-Sleeping Beauty, because even if she owned the magic mirror she would find a way to disbelieve its testimony. The Fairest of Them All rarely, if ever, knows she is so. She remains convinced that her ass or her breasts are too big or too small; that natural, charming asymmetries are uglinesses in need of chemical or surgical atten-tion; and that the positive testimonies of others are only flattery, kindness or indulgence.

Sally's different. Sally knows that she looks 'good enough.' Good enough, that is, to make male attentions problematic from time to time, on a scale of 'mildly irritating' to 'fucking annoying,' and good enough to make use of her looks if and when she finds it politic. More importantly, Sally looks 'good enough' for herself. She doesn't have any sense of needing anything more, is content with what she has.

She has reason for that, too. Anyone should be content, no

doubt, when they are truly blessed, but Sally's contentment, she has explained, goes beyond that.

"I love my body." The observation would sound narcissistic from almost anybody else.

"You should. You are so very beautiful." Safe ground, for me.

"Fuck that. The female body is beautiful. In the abstract, in the concrete, the female body is beautiful. Doesn't much matter, to me, what the proportions of the body are. Curve after curve, fat or thin, and the miracle of the cunt—all are beautiful.

"So many sensitivities, so many potential pleasures. 'Course, the fitter body gets the pleasure that comes from the chemistry of running or climbing, things like that, but look at the way women are made. How sensitive the skin is. How sensitive particular areas of skin are. The way the almost invisible hairs on our arms feel if we only brush them gently backward.

"We get aroused and blood flushes our nipples, our lips, cuntlips and cheeks. Little things, pretty things, sweet things, all flushing and growing at once, whilst all a man has is his fucking cock, made ponderous and foolish."

"Not just ponderous and foolish."

"Don't you defend them! You know that pisses me off."

"You're angry today."

"Yeah."

"Work?"

"Yeah."

She will have to tell it. She knows she will have to, but she is reluctant.

"Chapel Street," she says. "Fourth and Eldridge."

Working girls, then, almost certainly. I begin to stroke her flank, gently, glad of the heat that the rest of the world is cursing, because it means it is too hot for blankets and far too hot for sex under blankets, and I get to look at her endlessly naked.

"I hate Chapel Street." Her voice is sibilant with a darker passion than our own.

"I know."

"Just routine stuff, of course. Caspar and Weiner were there from Homicide. Izzy Morgenstein and di Matteo called it in."

"And the vic?"

"Some kid called Kassie. Short for Kassandra, spelled with a *K*."

"Black?"

"Yeah."

"Kassie who?"

"Whitney."

I try to remember, but the name means nothing to me.

"Dead?" The question is stupid, but we both know it's a prompt.

"Couldn't have been deader, poor kid."

"Got any idea who did it?"

"Warm when they found her. Jism still leaking from her cooch. Caspar's sure the DNA will be the killer's."

"She fucked unprotected?"

"Yeah. And her lipstick was kiss-smeared."

She is having a harder time with this than usual. Dead hookers are commonplace, scarcely making the inside pages anymore.

She rolls onto her back. Something that was smouldering low down inside me starts to sputter with flame. So confident, you see. Just lies there. Her arms are folded behind her head, her breasts spread that little extra by gravity, legs comfortably, revealingly parted. What is there is to die for.

"Todd was an asshole today."

"He was?"

"Yeah."

She's quiet, thoughtful, just gazing at the ceiling. The fan up

there rotates slowly, lazily. From low where I'm lying I can see
the length of her curving lashes, the bright highlights from the
window on the lenses of her eyes.

"I suspect he's not getting any." Her lips are tight. Bitter.

"He's married, isn't he?"

"Sure. To his college sweetheart."

"The cheerleader. Of course."

"Yeah. His fuckbunny." Her lip curls. I know all that shit
makes her mad. "I wish he'd grow up. Over thirty fucking years
old and his taste—really—is still for barely-post-pubescent-
looking kids in rah-rah skirts and shiny panties.

"He started cracking wise this morning. Making jokes. And
the thing is, there are jokes and jokes, you know?"

"Yes." It's amazing what some cops will laugh at, but that's
because there are times when it's only the ability to laugh at
something that keeps them going, that enables them to cope. A
lot of folks don't understand that.

It was as if she'd read my thoughts. "Just plain mean, his
jokes were, this morning. Just plain mean. You should have
seen Izzy's face. He's got kids, you know. Two girls, both about
Kassie's age.

"Todd really wound him up. Wound me up, too, the bastard.
If he goes on like this, I'm going to have to try to switch to
another partner."

"It's as bad as that?"

"Yeah. It's as bad as that. I'd say you should've heard him, but
I'm really awfully glad you didn't. Bastard. And it's something I've
noticed about him before. He hates hookers. With a passion."

"Probably his mother was one."

Sally laughs. It's a nicer sound.

"Fucking hypocrite."

"What?"

"Todd. Puts the squeeze on working girls any time he can. He likes to say, of sex, that he never has to pay for it. Fact is, that's only 'cuz he's good at squeezing freebies out of frightened youngsters."

I can see the change in her expression. There are things going on in her head that she hasn't given voice to. There's a passion that doesn't easily lend itself to words. Any moment and her eyes will moisten.

I love that in her. She is so very, very strong, so very, very confident. So very powerful. She speaks and others obey, her orders short and sharp as a whiplash, and there's scarcely a man in the precinct she couldn't knock down with a single punch. Still, though, injustice can move her to tears. And maybe the best part of that is that it means I get to baby her, to be part of making her feel better.

Her ankles move apart for me so that I can lie the length of her, my face level with her breasts. Her beautiful face above me.

The response is swift. I feel her groin thrust once, impulsively, and writhe just a little, nestling. Her nipples are flooding warm and blushing, quickly eager. I only need to breathe upon one and she moans very softly, to touch the moistness of my tongue to it and feel her catch her breath.

"Yes!"

What is the function of that word, I wonder. How superfluous it is when the body says the same so eloquently. I fill my mouth with her, tease one perking tip with ripples of my tongue while the fingers of my free hand find and gently work its sweet companion.

That upward pressure of her loins again, that subtle easing which, were she different, might bring other lips to her lips, a questing cock to her moistening cunt. Not this time though. Never, now, for her.

"Kiss…"

I am too eager to allow time for the full-formed phrase to escape her, bringing my mouth eagerly to hers, pressing the soft buttress of her lips with my own, finding her tongue with mine. A sweet confusion there, tongue on tongue. It is hard to know, at times, which tongue belongs to whom. And is hers really so long? It feels as if it could reach down into my belly.

No shuttle ever docked more closely upon an airlock. No breath escapes. Hers is mine and mine is hers, until it seems our lips are bruising and the de-oxygenated breath we share begins to tip us toward unconsciousness.

What a dizziness, what a fainting, this is…a gasping for air, because we cannot sustain the airlessness which is yet so delightful that we cannot easily part from it. A littler 'little death' than the one we hope will follow; still we cling to it.

Her breasts press against my own, matching softness to softness, smoothness to smoothness, nipples jousting gently, playfully. Her belly, too. Matchless in perfection, immeasurable in sweet fluency, pressing so perfectly, the simple senses of skin on skin heart-achingly lovely.

And I close my eyes to isolate that other sensation where mons rests on mons, both of us clean shaven, our two sacred mounds rubbing firmly on each other with every small yearning movement. I feel her hands pressing round the curves of my asscheeks, long slender fingers within teasing reach of that small, puckered ring, well-tended fingernails digging and sharp without, somehow, scratching.

Not wanting to break apart, intoxicated with shared breath, both of us know what we both want. Slippery already, the heat of the day and the heat of our wanting become a sweat-glaze on our eager flesh. I begin to slide down her, my tongue already hungry, and yet she prevents me.

No more than a pressure of fingertips, and ever so gentle at that, but still I know.

I lift myself lightly as she slides a little lower, and I reverse my position to kneel there, above her, and ease myself down. Her lovely thighs are parted above the naked pink vee of her, the sweet junction exposed as uncompromisingly as my own, which tingles to her gaze and the hope of her touch.

"Goddamn, you are beautiful."

In fact we say little. Those words are hers but could as easily have been mine. What I see is exquisite, and I know that what she looks upon is no less exquisite to her.

Within inches of her, I inhale her sweet perfume.

Oh, jeezus. So lovely. My chest aches with yearning. I moan, tears forming in my eyes, because I know she loves me so much. Her mouth warm, moist, closing around me... I close mine around her before I become too distracted.

We play mirrors. Each reflects back upon the other the sensations they feel. When her tongue describes a moist figure eight around my inflated outer lips, my tongue skates a parallel path round hers. Round and round, swirling, the both of us, and she who is 'mistress,' if only in persona, dips her tongue deep inside me and I follow her guide.

Not for the first time I wonder if I taste the same to her. I hope I do. She tastes like elixir. The magic juices emanating here are surely capable of miracles, the stuff of life.

Sweet smoothness slides upon my tongue inside her. Her tongue matches the motion and, again, the synchrony of movement and response is such that the sensation in my cunt could be the product of my own tongue. That is, perhaps, the joy of this, the miracle of fucking or being fucked by one of your own, so that you know what they are feeling.

My tongue presses deeper, as does her own, and my lips press firmly about that sacred site as if I would devour her. Between my thighs I feel what that is like, as if the hunger is hers, too. Only now the pressure's gone, nothing but a tongue tip left, flicking deftly at my clit. Oh, god, I may not believe in your existence, but there is no other name that springs so easily to my lips at such a time.

My hands press around her buttocks just as hers are pressing on mine, only cheekily, now, as I tease her own sweet nub, I let my index finger slide. Lubricious with sweat it slips within the ring, and I feel her start at the surprise of it. The quid pro quo is different though. No finger slides inside my ass, but her mouth closes small and tight around my clitoris, sucks rapidly and firmly till I would scream, if my mouth were not full.

I press my finger deeper, knowing that she likes it, and she acknowledges her gratitude, pushing and pressing her chin against my pubis as she begins to massage my cunt with long, hard tongue-licks. The flame within my belly surges as I know one must within her own. The chin upon my pubis, my own, now, upon hers, apes the movement and pressure of the pubic bone, driving us onward.

Sweat trickles across my breasts. Gentle rivulets flow down the valley of my ass. My chin begins to ache, and hers must as well. The fire in me roils and twists, a serpentine liquid madness of want and need and joy and glorious, nameless sensation.

A sudden surge and we are sliding sweat-soaked and laughing from the gorgeous peak, my lovely law-woman and I.

Afterward, an hour or two later, I watch her dress. Black shoes, blue pants, blouse and black-leather tunic, that absurdly— or is it wonderfully—masculine tie, the leather belt and deadly gun, the distinctive flat cap. I love to see her like that, not least because it reminds me every time of our first meeting.

I haven't quite succeeded in distracting her from what I wish she could forget.

"The first report I got was just of the death of a hooker," she says quietly, and I nod. Our understanding is unspoken.

"Be careful out there," I tell her. "Make sure you come home in one piece."

"You be careful, too. Very careful. You hear me?"

I nod again as she turns to go. I will, of course, be careful. I have a client arriving in twenty minutes or so, but I know him as I know all my customers, and I have little to fear. I have come a very long way from Chapel Street.

COP AT
MY DOOR

R. G. Emanuelle

B*ing-bong.*

"Well, here we go," I said, getting up from the couch.

Lisa got off the recliner and grinned.

"What are you smiling about? I don't enjoy opening up my door to find cops standing there. Nothing good ever comes from cops on doorsteps."

"Unless it's a really hot dyke cop. Then *lots* of good things can come of it." She giggled. If she hadn't been my best friend, I would have clobbered her.

I answered the door. "Hello, officers." I plastered a smile on my face, as Lisa always said I should. "Please come in."

The two police officers entered. One of them I'd never seen before. He walked in all business-like. As the other brushed past me, familiar stirrings in my lower belly began.

"Hi, Ms. Janssen," she said in that slightly gravelly voice of hers.

"Officer Brewer," I responded in a tone that suggested we'd

met before. And we had. Ever since I'd moved into this house, I'd had the pleasure of seeing this particular cop numerous times. While the reasons for our encounters were not amusing, I was secretly grateful for them.

"Officer Brewer," Lisa said in a saccharine-sweet voice. She was taunting me. "Where's your regular partner?"

"He's out on disability for a while. This is my temp partner, Officer Nolan."

Lisa and I nodded to Nolan, who was looking around the house, no doubt searching for crack pipes.

"I hope nothing bad happened to him," I said.

"No, just some minor surgery."

"You ladies both live here," Nolan said. It wasn't a question.

"Yes," I responded, looking only at him. I could tell that Brewer's eyes were fixed on me and if I looked at her, I'd collapse into a pile of goo.

"Your neighbor said you threw sticks at her."

"No, we didn't." There was still a serious matter to deal with. "They fell off the tree out front in the storm last night. She claims they're *my* branches, so she threw them over my front fence. So I just threw them back over to her side. Maybe she was standing too close."

Brewer put her hands around her utility belt, in a sexy Clint Eastwood-type stance.

"There's a history here of disputes," she said to Nolan. "The neighbor calls us out here pretty regularly." She looked at me again. When I caught sight of those amazing brown eyes, my muscles went limp and my underwear got damp.

Is it me, or do her eyes turn to liquid when she looks at me?

"Officer Nolan, could I speak with you privately?" Lisa called out from the kitchen. I hadn't seen her leave the room.

I turned to find Lisa standing on the threshold between the

kitchen and hallway, with a barely suppressed smirk. I threw her a "what are you doing?" look. She raised her eyebrows suggestively.

Nolan disappeared into the kitchen, and I was left standing there with Officer Hot-In-Her-Blues. Awkwardly, I turned back toward Brewer and attempted a smile. I'm sure it was pathetic. Brewer broke the silence.

"Look, I'll just say what I always say—try to keep out of her way and try to get along." I knew she knew that the bitch next door was crazy. Except that she couldn't actually say it.

"Uh, yeah." Lisa's voice ricocheted through my head: *Ask her out next time—and you know there'll be a next time.* She'd said it the last three times Brewer had come to the house. I didn't know if it was kosher to ask a police officer out while she was on duty. Maybe that was a big no-no. I didn't want to look like an idiot.

But with each visit from Officer Chocolate-Eyes, I reacted more strongly. At the moment, my stomach was tight, my knees were wobbly, and my clit was throbbing. And sweat gathered on my forehead. I prayed she couldn't see it. *So not sexy.*

"Hey, listen," I said. "You're really nice about coming here… I mean, I know you have to, but you're really nice about it." *That had to sound stupid.*

Thwarting my attempt—or perhaps rescuing me from it—Brewer's radio crackled with the voice of a dispatcher. She gripped the piece on her shoulder and tilted it toward her face, then inclined her head to speak into it.

"6-5 Adam. Still out. Leaving location. ETA about six minutes."

That. Was. So. Hot.

Brewer looked at me apologetically. Nolan came out of the kitchen, Lisa trailing him.

"Just try to get along," Nolan said to no one in particular.

"Some people just like to complain. Nothing you can do about it." He kept moving toward the door, passing Brewer on the way.

Brewer turned to follow him but stopped halfway and looked at me. "Till next time, I guess." The smile she gave me was sultry enough to steam the wrinkles out of my clothes—and then make them fall off.

"Make sure you bring the uniform. It does something for you." As soon as the words escaped my mouth, I wished I could fall through the cracks of my parquet floor.

And then Officer Brewer walked out of my door for the umpteenth time, leaving me wet and aching for her.

It was Saturday night and, as usual, I was alone. Lisa had gone off on a date, and I was settling in for an evening of old movies and "Saturday Night Live," a bucket of freshly popped popcorn on my lap. After my encounter with Officer Brewer that afternoon, I wanted to be alone, anyway.

The doorbell rang. I set my popcorn down and went to the door. When I opened it, I was surprised to find Officer Brewer on my doorstep. A sledgehammer to my gut would probably have had less impact.

"Hi," she said, quirking up one side of her mouth.

For a moment, I had a fantasy of the romantic suitor who just couldn't stay away from the object of her affection and came to serenade her at her door. But then I came crashing down to earth. This was a cop at my doorstep. *Nothing good ever comes from a cop on your doorstep.*

"Hi, Officer Brewer. Don't tell me my neighbor called you *again*? I haven't done anything since this afternoon."

Her lips quickly formed an "o" shape. "Oh, no, no. It's not that." Her lightly tanned, smooth face seemed to redden slightly under my porch light. She said nothing else, so I invited her in.

She stood stiffly in my hallway while I waited for her to explain her visit. Finally she cleared her throat. "I was on my way home and thought I should check in on you. I mean, you seemed upset earlier."

Oh. She's being a dutiful civil servant. "I'm fine. She's nuts." I waved my hand in the general direction of my neighbor's house. "Where's your partner?"

"He went home. We're off duty."

"Oh, right. You said you were on your way home." It was then that I noticed the lack of bulkiness in her shirt. No bullet-proof vest.

Wait a minute. She's off duty. "Do you often check in on people when you're off duty?" Despite my insecurity, I managed a flirty smile. I hoped I wasn't making a fool out of myself.

Brewer gave me a small smile in response. "No. I don't."

This statement completely dismantled me. Not the words so much as the look in her eyes as she said them. Those eyes, with their long, dark lashes, set above high cheekbones, told me that if I played my cards right, I'd find out what it was like to plunder the thin blue line. Problem was, I wasn't sure I believed it.

"Well, uh, since you were so kind to check in on me, the least I can do is offer you a drink. Wanna sit?"

"Sure." Brewer walked into my living room and sat down on the couch. I waited a moment before following her and stared at the back of her head. Her black hair was cut in typical dyke cop fashion—short on the sides, spiked up on top—although she did have a little swoop on the sides. I had the urge to sneak up behind her and slide my fingers through it. My fantasies about her had often included having my fingers in her hair while her head was between my legs.

I was jolted out of my thoughts when she turned around to look at me. "Um, are you going to join me in here, Ms. Janssen?"

"Oh, yeah. I was just going to ask you what you'd like to drink. And please, call me Morgan."

"Sure. Whatever you've got, Morgan."

I retrieved some wine from the refrigerator and brought it into the living room, along with two wineglasses. I uncorked the bottle and poured some out for each of us.

"Wow, I haven't seen rosé in a long time," she said, looking at the pink wine in her glass.

"Well, this is what rosé should be. I picked it up in Provence. They specialize in it there," I said, sticking my nose in the air in mock arrogance.

"Oh! I see." She flashed me another smile—a creamy white, beautiful smile. For a moment, I was bewitched.

We both laughed, then sipped.

"Mmm. This is good," she said.

"Told you."

Then there was an awkward silence. After a long minute, it was so painful that I had to end it.

"Were you worried that my neighbor snapped and beat me with that rake she's always using?"

Brewer laughed nervously. "Nah. People like that puff themselves up, but it's usually only for show, like a peacock." Then, after a pause, "I really just wanted to see you."

It may have been the lusty rosé, or it may have been the surreal quality of the moment, but I felt like a wave had picked me up off a beach and was holding me aloft on its crest, under a sparkling sun that warmed my skin from the inside out.

I decided it was the rosé and that I shouldn't get my hopes up too much. Officer Brewer was just being a concerned upholder of the law. I poured some more wine for both of us. "Oh, I'm fine. You don't have to worry about me." I gave the friendliest smile possible.

Brewer, on the other hand, got a strange look on her face, bringing her brows together ever so slightly. Like she was trying to figure something out.

"How did you—and Lisa, right?—come to live in this house together?" she asked.

"Long story short, I wanted a house but knew I couldn't pay all the bills myself, so I asked Lisa to move in with me and share the expenses. At least for a while, until I got things under control, got a raise at work, et cetera. It's working pretty well. Except for my crazy-ass neighbor."

"Yeah, unfortunately, I see this way too often. It's a shame." She sipped her wine and her eyes stopped at an art photo on the wall. Although she seemed taken with it, she didn't ask me about it. "So, what do you do?"

The conversation was in familiar territory now. Tucking my feet beneath me, I said, "I'm an X-ray technician."

"Sounds interesting."

"It's not."

Brewer laughed, hearty and unrestrained. It was deep and throaty and inviting.

The sun was making its final descent, and I lit a candle to keep the room softly lit.

"What's it like being a cop, Officer Brewer?" *Brilliant, original question.*

"Call me Nicole," she said. "It's a living." She lifted one eyebrow.

I wanted to ask her for stories but knew that sometimes cops didn't like to talk about "the job" when they were off duty, so I sipped as I tried to come up with alternative conversation topics. Then I thought, hell, she's sitting here in her uniform, and I have nothing to lose except my dignity.

"Why did you become a police officer?"

Her eyes were steady on mine. They were like hard, smooth stones, but in the shifting light of the room, they softened to warm, luminescent rings of sienna and sable.

"Because I sucked at everything else I tried."

I stopped mid-sip, not knowing if she was serious or joking. She grinned, and I swallowed. "You must have to go to a million places a day."

"I'm not one to sit behind a desk."

"I'm sorry," I said, suddenly self-conscious. "I don't mean to pry."

"That's okay. I don't mind."

In the span of time it took her to answer that question, I realized I'd come to care about Nicole Brewer. Not just lust for her, but care for her. And, as if I'd known her for years, I worried about her safety, physical and mental.

"Does it affect you? I mean in your head?"

Brewer gulped the rest of her wine. I held out the bottle to give her more. "No, thanks. I have to drive." She put her arm on the back of the couch and turned her body to rest one leg on the cushion. I could almost see the wheels spinning in her head trying to formulate her answer. I felt like I was being scrutinized.

"Not too many people think about that aspect of it," she said. "I love my job, but it's hard sometimes, like when you have to deal with brutality."

"But you don't see brutality every day, do you?"

"There's physical brutality, then there's brutality of the soul."

Whoa. Her eyes bore into mine, and I knew that she was entrusting me with something special and exclusive.

I felt honored. And guilty for objectifying her. Officer Brewer was not just a badge and uniform—hot as that was. She was a person, and she was a woman who probably cried now and then, even if only on the inside. When I finally got the gumption to speak, all I could say was, "Thank you for what you do."

Jesus, I sound like a dork. That was the most unsexy thing ever.

Her features softened into an array of emotions I wanted to study and dissect and understand. But not now. Right now, I was wet for her and wanted to do nasty things to her.

"Look, I should go," Nicole said, getting up. "I didn't mean to take up so much of your time."

Well, that's it. I blew it. I kept myself from leaping off the couch and grabbing her by her well-muscled shoulders. *Don't go!* "That's okay. I enjoyed talking to you."

As she walked to the door, I couldn't help but look at her ass. Even with the loose-fitting pants, I could see she was tight. *And round.*

Stop it! Stop it! I didn't want to be disrespectful. After all, she'd just bared her soul to me.

I wish she'd bare more.

Stop it!

She turned around and I just barely brought my eyes up to her face in time. If she'd caught me looking at her ass, I would've died.

"Thanks for the drink."

"My pleasure. Any time." *And don't forget the handcuffs. Oh, hell. Just the hat will do.*

I put my hand on the doorknob and hesitated. I really wanted her to stay, but I opened the door. She stood there looking at me for a moment. Again, I could see the wheels turning. But about what? What did she want to say?

"Take care," she said and walked out.

Once again, I'd let Officer Brewer walk out of my house, and all I had to show for it was a wet crotch.

* * *

Cats purred contentedly by my head on the sofa's back. I'd been sitting there for a while, thinking about Nicole, and finally decided to go to bed. After turning out the lights, I headed upstairs to my bedroom. I was just about to change when the doorbell rang.

I went back downstairs, a little freaked at first, considering it was one a.m. But by the time I got to the bottom, I'd decided that it was my crackpot neighbor ringing my bell to complain some more. Angrily, I flipped the switch for the porch light and pulled the door open. "What?" I yelled.

"Whoa. Sorry, I know it's late."

Under the harsh light of the lamp, Nicole's features were sharp and clear. She seemed startled but not terribly so. She'd probably seen much more violent reactions than that.

"Nicole. I'm so sorry. I thought you were my neighbor." My face got hot, and I looked down at her feet.

"That's okay. Is it too late?"

"No. Not at all. Come in." I held the door open and as she walked past me, I got a whiff of musk, and it went right to my clit. The pulsating began all over again. "Is everything okay?"

Nicole hung her head for a minute and she stared at the parquet floor, as if contemplating something. Her thumbs were hooked on her utility belt in that way I loved.

"Nicole?" I put my hand on her arm. Had something bad happened after she'd left earlier?

Before I could register anything, Nicole turned fully toward me, pushed me against the corridor wall and kissed me. As stunned as I was, it didn't take long for me to fall into her kiss and let my lips part for her. Her hands went around my waist, and I slid my palms up the well-ironed blue shirt, my ring catching on the edge of her NYPD patch. When both my hands were behind her neck, she held me tighter and pressed her full weight onto me. Her kisses became harder, more urgent, and her tongue slipped into my mouth hungrily. She pulled away, breathing heavily.

I'd fantasized about this woman so much, and now that I had her in my arms and had felt her lips on mine, I didn't know what to do. So, I opened my mouth to speak. "Is that a gun in your pocket or are you just happy to see me?"

She let out a sputtering laugh. I laughed, too. "Sorry, I've always wanted to say that."

"It's okay." She chuckled again.

The evening was warm and muggy, and the house offered little air. I wiped a bead of sweat from my temple. "Hey, you wanna step outside to my backyard? It's cooler out there."

"Sure."

I led the way to the back of the house, the whole time self-conscious about my backside. Was she looking at it? Did it look good? Was it jiggling? I was relieved when we'd gone through the door, and I was able to move to the side. I flipped on the back porch light. When I turned, she was looking at me with such intensity that I thought I would spontaneously combust.

I swallowed hard. "Um, we can sit over here," I said, pointing to a stone bench. I sat, but she remained standing.

My garden was my oasis, a place of Zen tranquility. Fruit trees rose to meet the ten-foot fence surrounding my backyard. Fallen peaches dotted the grass, and the little plums that had gotten too ripe left wine-colored blotches on the paving stones.

"Wow, this is really nice." Brewer pulled her eyes off me to look around at my creation.

"Thanks. I love it out here. It keeps me sane."

"Too bad your neighbor is nuts." She turned to me and smiled. "That's off the record, of course."

"Of course." *Would throwing you to the ground, ripping your uniform off, and making your eyes roll to the back of your head be off the record, too?*

"What are these for?" she asked, pointing to a pile of canvas.

"Oh, those were on my furniture. Haven't put them away yet."

Nicole didn't respond and instead strolled around my garden, casually looking at the flowers and bushes, gently squeezing a fig on my fig tree. The fruit was ripe and popped easily, sending honey-thick nectar down Nicole's hand.

"Oh, wow, I'm sorry," she said. "I didn't mean to do that."

"That's okay. There's plenty more."

Nicole looked at her hand and brought it up to her mouth. She looked at me and sensuously licked the juice from her hand. The way her tongue slid across her skin, that's how I wanted her tongue to slide through my pussy, catching my juices. *Jesus, I might come right now.*

Nicole standing there in her uniform, her hand wet and her eyes dark with desire, sent my insides out of control and, despite the heat, goose bumps tracked my arms.

Nicole went to the tarps and picked one up, then walked over to me. Thinking that she wanted to sit, I scooted over a little more. But as I turned my head upward, she threw the tarp down and knelt on it. The little NYPD pins on her shirt collars glinted in the lamp light in my yard, and I stared at them as she reached up to undo my shorts. I looked around with a little panic but relaxed when I realized that my neighbors could not see us, thanks to the high fences.

My shorts and underwear were now on the ground. The stone bench felt hard but cool under my butt. As her fingers skimmed the inside of my thighs, my skin prickled and I prayed that it didn't make any hair on my legs stand up.

When her hands reached the top of my thighs, she reached around to my buttocks and yanked me forward. Taken a little by surprise by her forcefulness, I lost my balance and started to fall backward, but my hands instinctively went behind me and caught the back edge of the bench.

She lifted my legs so that the backs of my thighs rested on her shoulders and my heels flanked her ribs. I was now literally at the edge of my seat, knees in the air, and Nicole's face was descending. I closed my eyes and waited to feel her tongue in my pussy, but it seemed like I was waiting, and waiting. I opened my eyes to see her looking up at me with a smirk. She was torturing me, but I knew it was only to assert control. I could see how she probably made a great cop.

Finally, she lowered her head and her tongue made contact with my clit. My head fell back and I let out an "ahh" as I crooked my arms and leaned back on my elbows.

Her tongue circled around, skirted off to the sides, glided along the edges of my lips, then tickled my hole. It stiffened and slid inside me. Nicole tongue-fucked me for a while before coming back up to my clit.

As she lapped me, she lightly brushed my entrance with her index finger. Then two fingers. Then she slid them in. She sucked and fucked me simultaneously, and I could feel my wetness coating her cheeks as her face grazed my thighs, first one side then the other. Her other hand reached up, skimmed over my stomach and underneath my tank and bra. She cupped my breast and squeezed. I moaned some more.

Her thrusts got harder and faster, and she sucked on my clit, hard beneath her luscious tongue. Little explosions began in my belly and grew until I was almost breathless. The sensation rolled through me, taking over my muscles and veins, until my orgasm would not be contained any longer.

Throughout my shuddering, I clamped my jaw shut, even though low guttural sounds escaped my throat. I couldn't be too loud because if my neighbor found out what I was doing, she'd call the cops and complain about indecent exposure or something. That's all I needed. Little did she know that the cop who usually responds to her complaints was between my knees sucking me off.

Nicole's fingers retreated and I heard a slight slurping sound as she pulled her face away. She wiped her cheeks on my thighs, gently brought my legs down and stood up. Her uniform had not suffered in the slightest from our carnal encounter. I, on the other hand, was completely disheveled. My shorts and underwear were in a heap, my shirt was pushed up over my breasts and I was soaked. I pushed myself up into a sitting position and caught my breath. Nicole was looking at the fence separating my property from my crazy neighbor's.

"What are you doing?" I asked.

"Just looking to see if there are any spaces where your neighbor could look in."

"No, it's pretty tight." *Thank god.*

I walked over to where she stood and turned her around. I pushed her up against the wooden fence, put my arms around her neck and kissed her. My tongue easily slid through her red, swollen lips, and I tasted myself on her tongue. I moved my hands down her chest, over the pins, over her NYPD badge and name tag, across her hard nipples, down to her pants. It occurred to me, briefly, that she'd removed her utility belt. *Too bad. That might have been interesting.*

Once I'd unbuckled her belt, I undid her pants and lowered the zipper. Still kissing her, I slid a hand inside her underwear. I so craved to feel her warm, wet pussy on my face that I just pulled her pants down and knelt in front of her. "Spread 'em,"

I said, in imitation of cop theatrics, and kissed her in her center. She was slick and felt smooth on my lips.

"Wait, wait," she said breathily. She moved over a few inches to get her back off a decorative butterfly I'd nailed to the fence. I stood up, moved over to stand in front of her, then unbuttoned her shirt and pulled her sports bra up to release her breasts. Her nipples were hard and fleshy between my teeth, and I could feel her squirming under my ministrations. Her hat was on a chair and I bent to pick it up. I put it on her head. She looked puzzled for a moment, then a bemused smile lit her face.

Working my way down again, I licked her salty, sweaty skin. Her tight stomach quivered when I kissed it, and she let out a broken sigh when I finally slipped my tongue into her pussy. Closing my eyes helped me dissolve into the pleasure of eating out Officer Nicole Brewer. I felt her move and opened my eyes. She slid down slightly, anchored her back against the fence, which spread her wider and gave me more to look at, more to lick. I crouched all the way down onto my heels and inched my way closer so that I was directly beneath her, my knees on her pants. With my head tilted up, I covered her with my mouth.

She began grinding into my face and pushing my head harder into her pussy. My neck started to protest, and it felt like it would break. But I didn't care. *What a way to go.* Maybe if I were naughty enough, she'd cuff me.

Her blue shirt hung open, covering half of each breast to the nipples, her badge golden in the light. The hat was tilted down, shadowing her eyes. Rivulets of sweat trickled down her temples, and a light sheen covered her cheeks. *God, she is so fucking hot!*

I ran my palms up her thighs and latched onto her hips. As she moved harder and faster against my face, I gripped her and pulled her down even harder. Her hands left my head to find purchase on the fence behind her. Fingernails scratched the wood slats, and that was the only sound as Nicole came hard but quietly. Totally in control.

When she finished, I pulled away and licked my lips. A sharp pain in my neck kept me from straightening my head for a minute, but when I finally did, the pain gave way to euphoria. The woman I'd fantasized about for months was finally mine and her essence was on my face, cooling in the slight night breeze that had picked up. Nicole adjusted her pants, then helped me up.

"Yum," she said with a satisfied smile.

"Definitely."

A thought occurred to me. Now that I'd had my fantasy woman, what next? Now that I'd tasted her, felt her, I wanted more. I didn't know what to do once I'd adjusted my clothes. So I looked around but watched from the corner of my eye as she fixed her bra and buttoned her shirt. She plucked off her hat, wiped her forehead, ran her hand through her hair and put the hat back on.

With her hands around my waist, she pulled me to her. We had to tilt our heads at sharp angles because of the hat, but it was worth the crick in my neck. Our kiss was warm and moist and infused with the flavors of our desire.

"I'd like to see you again," she said.

My head almost exploded, and a wild pleasure swept through me.

"I thought you'd never ask." Standing there with Nicole, dark and formidable, I took a mental snapshot. I wanted to always remember how she looked at that moment. Nicole in a uniform was better than any other woman naked.

"But will you wear the uniform for me again, Officer Brewer?"

"Ah, I shouldn't have worn it this time. I'm off duty."

"Why did you?"

She smiled devilishly. "Because you essentially said that it turns you on."

My face got hot again. "Well, I'll take you any way you come."

"Hmm, I like the sound of that."

"Mmm hmm. Just keep responding to those complaints." I smiled.

Nothing good ever comes from a cop on your doorstep? Only if the cop comes in...and comes.

TORN OFF
A STRIP

Elizabeth Coldwell

It's quiet for a Friday night, rain seeming to keep even the lowest of the lowlifes off the streets. Hawkes and I are getting takeout coffee and donuts from the diner on Main Street when the call comes in. Some kind of disturbance at a party, from what I can make out over the static. It's a familiar story: the neighbors had been willing to ignore the loud music and general rowdiness till they heard what sounded like female screams and punches being thrown; then they got alarmed and called us.

"It'll be nothing," Hawkes grumbles, sliding back behind the wheel of the patrol car. Seems to me like it's a little more of a squeeze for him than it used to be, and maybe he should do something about that burgeoning gut of his. I could say something, but he never really takes advice from his Aunty Pamela, as he insists on calling me even though the guy's only a couple of years younger than I am. "Damn waste of our time going over there, if you ask me."

"Well, as long as they keep paying us to waste our time like this..." I'm not quite as cynical as Hawkes, even though I've spent more than enough time on the beat to have all the idealism of my rookie years burned clean away. I still see some good lurking in the average citizen, though I sometimes wish they'd make more of an effort to sort out their own petty domestic disputes before turning to us for help.

The address given to us by the dispatcher is in a nice suburb, on a street of small, wood-framed houses painted in cute pastel shades. It reminds me of the street I lived on as a kid. Though, growing up, I never saw a sight quite like the one that greets Hawkes and me as we step out of the patrol car into the downpour. A blonde, handcuffed to the porch railing. She's dressed in a uniform which, I realize as we near her, is a costume-shop fantasy version of the one I'm wearing. As many shirt buttons have been fastened up as can offer her a veneer of respectability, but her big tits are straining to be free of their confinement, and her thigh-high stockings are ripped in a couple of places. Close up, she can't be more than twenty-one, twenty-two at the most, the last traces of puppy fat still filling out her heart-shaped face. There's a half-inch of black roots visible in her tangled, peroxided bob. She's a spitting, cursing, furious mess, and just the sight of her sets a pulse beating hard and fast between my legs.

"Thank god you're here, Officer," a woman is saying to Hawkes. She has rollers studded in her mousy hair and a face pinched from lack of sleep, and I assume she's the one who called in the complaint. She stares at the blonde with a look of fierce distaste as she shelters under her umbrella. "Should have known when we saw the little hussy arrive she'd be trouble."

It's easy to picture the woman peering through the slats in her blinds to check who's ringing next door's doorbell, nosiness masked with a thin veil of neighborly concern. Sometimes her type are a help; more often they're just a hindrance.

"I think we can take it from here," Hawkes replies. He turns his attention to the group of five or six young men who emerged from the house at his knock. A couple are shirtless, and most of them are clutching beer cans. That, combined with the disordered look of a house where a bunch of guys live without a regular female presence, tells me all I need to know about the party taking place here.

"Does someone who was in the house want to tell us what actually happened?" I ask, anxious to stamp some authority on a situation that still threatens to get out of hand.

Hawkes glares at the neighbor till she gets the message that she isn't needed anymore, and she shuffles off in fluffy mules, somewhat bedraggled by now, back to her own house.

"They're keeping me against my will," Blondie pipes up, only to be roundly ignored.

"Look, Officer—er—Farley." One of the shirtless guys, with the look of a surfer dude who's somehow found himself stranded a thousand miles from the nearest ocean, reads my name off my shirt. He's slurring a little, but he's still pretty lucid. I've had to make sense of much worse before now. "We were throwing a bachelor party for my brother, Joel, and we hired her—" he throws a contemptuous gesture in the direction of the handcuffed blonde, "to provide a little entertainment, you know?"

One of his buddies starts chipping in, talking over the top of him. Beer does that, makes you loud and self-important, though the way he's attempting to force himself center stage makes me think he's always seen himself as alpha frat boy. Through the jumble of conversation I pick out the gist of the story. Blondie arrived at ten, as arranged, and went through a strip routine to some old Def Leppard number that had all the guys drooling. When Surfer Dude describes how she'd rubbed her big, bare tits all over his brother's face, I think he's damn near going to come in his shorts. Thinking about the scene has my own juices trickling into my panties, even though I'm doing my best to stay professionally detached.

After that, she'd been persuaded to go upstairs with the bachelor boy, though from the way they tell the story, she didn't need much in the way of persuading. She sucked his cock a little, fucked him every which way, waited till she thought he'd fallen asleep—then lifted his wallet. He'd seen her but hadn't been quick enough to stop her leaving the room. Surfer Dude and Alpha Frat, alerted by Bachelor Boy's yelling, grabbed her as she tried to leave the house. Cue a furious altercation that ended with Blondie being fastened to the porch rail with the cuffs she'd brought as part of her outfit and the phone call bringing us here.

"It'll teach me to do a bit more research next time," Surfer Dude finishes up. "Not just hire some chick who leaves her number on the wall by the pay phones in McMullen's."

Throughout all of this, Blondie continues to protest her innocence, though she'd be better off saving her breath. I've got her pegged. Strictly amateur hour, doing a saucy little strip show here and there to help pay her way through college. Too young to realize that robbing the guy you've just fucked, particularly when all his friends are partying downstairs, isn't the most sensible way to make an extra few bucks on top. The way Surfer Dude is talking, at least a couple of them would have gladly paid for a helping of what Joel, the groom-to-be, had just had.

But maybe once was quite enough for her. They say all strippers have daddy issues, but I can tell that isn't true in Blondie's case. From the way I've caught her looking at me, desire and confusion blazing in her big brown eyes, she is clearly struggling to deal with the fact she's more attracted to women than men, and she hasn't yet figured out what to do about it.

I know all she needs is a little guidance, a little help from someone who's already walked that same path, and I'm just the woman to give it to her. I look at Hawkes, scribbling something in his notebook, and a wicked thought occurs to me. It means crossing a line, taking a risk that could see me thrown out of the police department if I'm caught, but I can't help myself. The sight of her, restrained and ready to burst ripely out of that slutty costume, taps into every dark, dirty fantasy I have when I lie in bed at night and run my pocket rocket vibrator over my clit.

I tap Hawkes on the shoulder. "Tell you what, why don't you take the guys inside and start getting more coherent statements from them while I get Blondie's side of the story?"

He doesn't look thrilled, knowing it's going to take him a while to get even one version of the story straight, but he nods and starts to usher the revelers inside. When they're all safely out of the way, I turn my attention to Blondie.

"Okay, let's see what we've got here." Standing close to her, she smells of sex and some cheap dime-store perfume. It's an enticing combination, one I could breathe in for a while. "Why don't you start by telling me your name?"

"Vixen." When I stifle a laugh, she pouts at me. "I'm telling you, it's Vixen Molloy. Check my ID. It's in my breast pocket. I'd get it out for you, but…" She gestures to her bound wrists. She's not being outright hostile, but there's a challenge underlying her words.

Just as there's a challenge in fishing her ID out of the cheaply tacked-on shirt pocket. Through the thin fabric I can feel the warmth, the softness of her breast, taunting me with its nearness. I retrieve the laminated card and squint at it. Sure enough, she's called Vixen. I suppose it saved her the problem of deciding on a stripper name.

I turn my attention to the cuffs that have been used on her.

A quick examination reveals them to be the kind you can buy in any adult toy store. "The keys to these things, they in your pocket, too?"

She shakes her head. "One of the guys took them. Said he'd hand them over to the cops when they arrived."

"Okay, so it looks like you're not going anywhere for a while." I glance at the neighboring windows, all shuttered and dark now that the excitement has died down. "Suits me. I can do what I have to do here."

"And what do you have to do, exactly?" Again that little hint of defiance. Just enough of the brat about her to have me creaming as I think about spanking her ass till she learns how to show due respect to an officer of the law.

"Pat you down. Make sure you haven't lifted anything else from the house."

She shakes her ratty blonde head. "Uh-uh. Just the wallet. I thought I could get out of there before he even noticed it was gone."

"You've got a lot to learn, sweetie." Quickly, efficiently, I pat down her flanks from behind as I read Vixen her rights. It's just a cursory search. That costume is so damn skimpy there's nowhere to hide anything without it being immediately obvious. Still, this all has to be done, even if only to scare her off trying anything so idiotic in the future.

My hands brush over her boobs, even though I've already established there's nothing in the pocket there but her ID and a couple of folded bills, her fee for tonight's performance. As I feel her nipples, jutting out to meet my touch, any pretense I have that this is simply a routine search fades away. Before she can say a word, I pop open the buttons on her shirt and her bare tits fall out into my hand.

She doesn't protest as I lovingly knead the firm, creamy flesh, even though she'd be perfectly at liberty to yell blue murder till Hawkes came dashing out to catch me fondling her. What I'm doing is so inappropriate, but it feels so right. A squall of rain catches me in the face as the wind changes direction, but it doesn't cool me down or bring me to my senses. All I can think about is the way Vixen's nipples are pushing against my palms, almost seeking to bore their way through my skin.

She wants this just as badly as I do, that much is evident. Her ass is pushing back against me, the metal cuffs rattling rhythmically against the wooden railing as she gyrates. My pussy is heating up, pressing against the seam of my uniform pants and setting up the most delicious friction as I move.

"I'm in trouble, aren't I, officer?" Vixen's voice is huskily insolent, goading me on.

No, you *are* trouble, I want to reply, but my hand is already flipping up the hem of her skirt in my impatience to strip her further. The thong back of her panties is so thin it barely conceals her asshole, and her shaven lips bulge out around it, demanding to be stroked. I push the cheap scarlet lace to one side, skating a fingertip over her wet folds.

Somewhere close by, a car engine starts up. I freeze, wondering if we're about to be spotlighted on the porch, caught in the act, but the driver passes by without bothering to switch on his headlamps. Any other time, any other place, my first instinct would be to follow him and dish out a ticket, but I'm too busy breathing a sigh of relief to bother about that now.

"Where were we?" I murmur. "Oh, yeah..." I return to my gentle exploration of Vixen's pussy lips. "So, if I put my fingers in you, are they going to come away all sticky with Bachelor Boy's come?"

She shakes her head vigorously. "I used a condom, Officer. Spare me the safe-sex lecture. I'm not stupid."

"Really? You try to steal a guy's wallet when he's got a houseful of buddies to catch you as you leave. Sounds pretty stupid to me. And now you've let yourself get chained up and stripped half-naked…"

"But I'm being punished, aren't I, Officer?" Again that submissive tone to her voice, sending another little gush of juice into the crotch of my sensible cotton underwear. She's almost taunting me to spank her ass. If it weren't for the fact that I can hear a hubbub of voices and laughter from inside the house, telling me the boys might have been a little more helpful than Hawkes or I expected, I'd punish her till those sweet little cheeks of hers bore the red marks of my palm. As it is, I settle for a swift, hard swat to each one, bringing a noise from her that's somewhere between a yelp and a satisfied moan.

Then my fingers push up into her wetness, into the cunt that's already welcomed the groom-to-be's cock tonight. When he entered her, did she sigh the way she's sighing now? Did she thrust her rump at him and beg for more, like she's asking—pleading—for me to touch her clit? She looks back over her shoulder at me, mascara-streaked eyes full of desperation and horniness. For a moment, I make her think I'm going to do what she wants, but I can't let her forget who's in control here. My thumb settles on her asshole instead, rubbing in little back-and-forth motions that make her jerk like she's wired up to the mains.

"You like that, do you?"

She tries to shape a reply, but when I switch my attention to her clit, circling it relentlessly, her words turn into incoherent gasps and gulps. The brattiness, the defiance is gone; she's just a soft, pliant mess of girl-flesh, completely in my thrall.

I've got her pinned against the railing, my thigh over hers so that as she bucks against me, the pressure is stimulating me in just the right place. What I could really use is Vixen's wet little tongue working away between my legs, but that's not going to happen, so I settle for subtly rubbing against her leg.

She's close, so very close now, and my fingers are slipping and sliding in the wetness that pours like rain from her. The open front of her slutty cop outfit flaps in the night air. Her little whimpers are driving me crazy. "Come for me," I order her, fighting to keep the authority in my voice till the end. Her cunt convulses around my fingers, at the same time as a sweet, sharp orgasm ripples through my belly. I know I'll replay this moment over in my head once I'm off shift, turning myself on all over again with the sight and sound of Vixen coming on my command.

A door slams in the house, bringing me back to full awareness of where I am. By the time Hawkes and the party boys spill out of the house, I've got Vixen all buttoned up and respectable once more. Surfer Dude fishes the handcuff keys out of his shorts pockets and, finally, she's released.

"All sorted?" I ask Hawkes.

"Yeah. Joel here's decided not to press charges, seeing as how no real harm's been done." He's making it clear this whole incident has been a waste of our time, just as he predicted when we answered the call. His time, maybe. Not mine.

"Great, saves us the paperwork." I look out at the steadily falling rain, then back to Vixen in her insubstantial outfit. Her face glows with satisfaction and more, as though I've helped her come to a realization about who she is and what she needs to make her whole. "I was thinking, we should give Ms. Molloy a lift home. Make sure she can't get into any more trouble tonight."

"Sure, whatever," Hawkes replies without enthusiasm. I can tell he'd prefer this not to be his problem, already starting to look forward to the end of our shift and whatever his wife's preparing for his breakfast.

As we're walking back to the patrol car, I say to Vixen,

"Well, I hope you learned your lesson tonight. But don't let me catch you prancing around pretending to be a policewoman again." Bending close to her ear, speaking so low that Hawkes won't be able to hear, I add, "On the other hand, if you ever feel the need to dress up as a slutty nurse, maybe we can work something out."

OFFICER BIRCH

J. N. Gallagher

I can't believe you made me wait twelve years, Officer Birch. No, I'm not going to call you Melissa, or Mel. I don't care what your friends call you. We are not friends anymore. Whatever we are, whatever this is, is not a friendship.

Yes, I will always be thankful for what you did. You were the first person, ever, who stood up for me. It doesn't change anything, but if I never said the words, I should have. Thank you.

I'll bet Rachel Winston still regrets choosing your first day on the job to bash my head against the hallway lockers. I don't remember much, but I do have a reliable report of what happened. Here's part of a note my friend Amy wrote me the next day:

> *You crumpled and people started walking around you. Rachel was laughing and walking away, and all of a sudden the new resource cop chick came*

*running down the hall. Everyone scattered, and when
the cop got to Rachel, she took that fucking bitch
down hard! She had her in handcuffs in two seconds.
Rachel started crying, but the cop (who looks like a
major lesbian and I'll bet is into some really hard-core
dyke sex shit) dragged Rachel down the hallway, and
another cop came and took her. They brought you
to the nurse's office, and the cop asked if Rachel had
hurt you before. I snorted because Principal Dickface
was in there, and he knows about all the shit Rachel's
done, but then Dickface made me leave.*

Later that day, you called me into your office for a meeting. I
didn't know what we were supposed to talk about. I remember
that, as you formally introduced yourself, I was staring at your
boots, all shiny and black and *tap-tap-tapping* the floor.

You asked if Officer Rackers had done anything about
Rachel's bullying. Of course he didn't. No one did. They sent
her to detention a couple of times, but that was it. Her dad was
president of the school board. The principal was scared of her.

"Why does she bully you?" you said. "From what I've gathered, she doesn't act violently toward anyone else."

"I don't know," I said. "Does there have to be a reason?
Sometimes people here just get singled out, and we have to deal
with it."

You were silent until I lifted my head and looked at you. Did
you know that I fell in love with you right then, Officer Birch?
Could you tell?

It might have been your uniform, immaculate and wrinkle-
free. It might have been the necktie and cap, which no cops
in town wore until you showed up and made them look like
slobs.

It might have been your face. You looked so young, almost my age. Let's be honest—you weren't pretty. You weren't cute, either, not like the few girls I had managed to fool around with. They had long hair, beautiful breasts, curves to their figures. You had sharp angles, small breasts, a strong jaw. I didn't know if you had hair on your head. I couldn't see any peeking out from under your cap.

I had seen butch women before. Our midwestern county was closeted back then but not totally straight. The difference was that none of them were anything like you. So handsome, so powerful in your uniform, even while sitting down and doing nothing. Masculine in every way yet nothing like a man. I got moist right there, and I didn't even know I was attracted to butches.

You rambled on about handling bullies. I wasn't listening; I was thinking. What would it be like to kiss your lips? What was underneath your cap? How would you teach me about *hardcore dyke sex shit*?

Then you put your hand on my knee. That got my attention.

"Rachel is not going to bother you anymore," you said. "Do you understand? This is 1998. We're almost at a new century, and we're not going to let the same crap keep happening. If it does, she's not going to be here. I'm going to watch out for you."

I nodded. Your eyes showed genuine compassion, and I believed you.

I only volunteered as a D.A.R.E. speaker to be around you. I admit that. However, I think I deserve some credit in that I never flirted with you or said anything inappropriate. I know I mentioned I had turned eighteen the summer before senior year a thousand times, but that was just to let you know I was a legal adult, and it was okay to be attracted to me. You sure talked to me a lot, more than any of the other volunteers. I hoped the reason was because you liked tall, awkward, sort-of-pretty brunettes with medium-sized breasts, though I figured it was because I was totally clean and the other volunteers weren't. They were lying to little kids to pad their scholarship applications.

Honestly, I did enjoy talking to younger students. I also enjoyed watching you on the job. You didn't try to be cool or everybody's friend. You just wanted to help people and uphold the law. That's cool all by itself, and it made me want to fuck you even more.

I had to be ready for you. The other girls had been gentle, but you didn't seem like a gentle person. I needed an idea of what was waiting for me. I could have hooked up with someone on the Internet, but that seemed dangerous. I couldn't find anything good online because we only had one computer, in the living room, with a porn filter I never did crack.

I'm still surprised I gathered enough courage to visit one adult video store, let alone two or three. Nobody had what I needed. They had plenty of bleached-blondes eating each other out, but the ecstasy on the box covers was so fake, I laughed out loud.

One cashier, a guy in his late thirties, noticed I had been wandering around. He politely offered assistance. I described what I was looking for, and he said there was a lesbian book-store about five hours away, across the state line, that carried smut. He called the owner, asked what she had in stock, and told me, "She'll ship some stuff here, or you can drive up there if you'd like."

I wasn't going to wait. I told my parents I was staying with Amy and needed to borrow our VCR because hers was broken. I reserved a room at a Super 8 near the bookstore. I wasn't going to make a ten-hour round trip, and I didn't know when I'd be home alone to watch the stuff.

Close your eyes and imagine: me, lying on a king-size bed at a Super 8, lights off, curtains closed and a remote control in my left hand.

I know you've seen the tapes and don't need me to rehash them, but I wonder what you felt the first time you saw them. Were you as moved as I was, Officer Birch? I didn't know two femmes would ever spank each other hard enough to leave large welts on their asses for fun. I felt warm when a thin woman wearing a realistic dildo with balls made romantic love to a beautiful red-headed babe. I watched a supposed real-life couple have sex and then kiss and cuddle for fifteen minutes. And I almost ruined one tape rewinding to the scene where a dyke with messy hair named Al was gagged, tied naked to a barber's chair, and forced to endure a vibrator as her butch barber barked "Sit still!" while giving Al a precise flattop.

These tapes weren't meant to be bestsellers. They were labors of love. They didn't have porn stars in them, just regular women with regular bodies expressing their sexual selves. When I say they moved me, I mean in the same way we can be moved by a painting or a poem or a piece of music. Am I comparing porn to Mozart? Yes, I am.

My parents started attending church stuff at night, so I rubbed myself raw that first week. I even wrote a story about Al with the flattop and an unnamed, stocky butch from another tape who I called Joey. I wrote it down in a journal with a lock. Prior to this story, the journal made no mention of my being a lesbian, because I was afraid my parents might pick the lock. Here's an excerpt (remember, I was eighteen):

Joey, stocky with shaggy hair, grabbed Al, baby-faced with a flattop, and pushed her to the ground. Joey unzipped her jeans and pulled out her dick, which in reality was a dildo. It looked very much like a penis except that it was blue.

"Suck it," Joey said, commandingly.

Al sucked it good. Joey ran her fingers through Al's hair, or lack thereof. Al's head was shaved totally bald on the sides and had but a small, boxy sculpture on top. Al took the dildo into her mouth as far as she could, but it was not far enough for Joey. Not nearly enough.

"Deeper. I want to hear you gag."

Al did take it deeper, which made her gag for almost four seconds, and then Joey mercifully pulled the dildo out of Al's mouth. Al had drool and spit coming off of her lips. Then Joey ordered Al to take off her pants. Al did and stood there in boxers. Joey wasn't satisfied. Al removed the boxers to reveal her dildo and harness.

"Take off your dick, too," Joey stated.

"No," Al said.

"You're my boy if I want you to be, and you're my girl if I want you to be," Joey implored.

Al sighed, then did as she had been told to do. Joey forced her to the ground. They were in an automobile repair shop. Al was on the cold concrete floor, and she spread her legs, grudgingly, so that Joey could get a good look at her pussy.

"Get ready," Joey said.

She climbed on top of Al and started fucking her pussy. Al moaned with pleasure. Her moans were quizzical, like she was not expecting to enjoy being fucked.

"Oh?" Al exclaimed. "Oh, god!"

"Yeah, baby," Joey said while she kept thrusting and grinding deeper and deeper into Al's pussy. The dildo moved in and out seemingly hundreds of times.

Suddenly, Joey pulled out the dildo and told Al to flip over. Joey reached her hand down into the wetness of Al's slit, and then spread a glob of that into Al's asshole. Then, the dildo slid inside Al's asshole. Al gasped as it went all the way in.

"Oh!" Al said.

"Take it, baby," Joey said. "Take the whole damn thing."

I wrote that story in honor of the videos, where some butches were stone, some liked to be touched and some liked to be fucked. I also realized that watching pornography wasn't enough to learn about you or about myself. I spent hours hiding in corners at the public library, which had a surprising number of gay and lesbian books. Our Internet filter might have stopped porn, but it didn't block nonexplicit literature on lesbian sexuality. I didn't just jerk off, Officer Birch. I did my homework, too.

I went straight to your house after my graduation ceremony, one of only a few students who didn't attend the all-night lock-in. I knew you would be home. After our last D.A.R.E. presentation, you told me on the ride back that you were staying in. The reason you had been assigned to the school was because no one else would do it, and you hadn't anticipated how much stress there would be. You were burned out.

I didn't know if that was a coded invitation. I didn't really care. I was going to show up at your house at some point. Why not make it a night when I was dolled up? When I was wearing a tight black dress (covered by a gown for most of the evening) and a pair of my mom's heels.

I remember ringing your doorbell, trying desperately to fix my graduation-cap hair. You opened the door wearing cut-off jeans, a Chicago Cubs T-shirt and a Cubs hat. You looked so delicious, I was ready for anything you might want to do to me.

But you just stood in the doorway and asked if something was wrong.

"Everything's fine," I said. I attempted to look smoldering, but I'm sure my smile was crooked and my *come-hither* expression was laughable.

"Did something happen between you and Amy? Did you guys have a fight?"

"What?"

"Look," you said. "I didn't think it was appropriate to talk about, but you're a graduate now." You paused for a moment. "I know you're a dyke, and you know that I'm one, too."

"How could you know a thing like that?" I said. "Do I act gay? Do I look gay?"

You smiled, and I wanted to melt in your arms.

"We can just tell, sometimes. I've seen how you look at other girls. Please, tell me if I'm wrong."

"You're not," I said. "But Amy's not gay. We're only friends. I am ready, though, for a real relationship. I'm eighteen. I'm ready for more adult stuff."

You still didn't invite me inside. You started talking about lesbian relationships, and then you were off in lecture-land. *Hope for the future. Gay marriage someday.* You weren't even looking at me. You tilted your head to the sky, and you looked at the street behind me, and you looked down at your front porch. Not at me.

I've experienced agony in my life, Officer Birch, but nothing has come close to how I felt when you reached out and squeezed my shoulder, the same way my dad and uncles did. That confirmed I wasn't special. I was just another student in the crowd. Nothing dirty or kinky was ever going to happen.

I began to cry, slow tears at first and then an overflow. Snot dripped all over my dress. You withdrew your hand. I fished around in my purse for an envelope with *Officer Birch* written on the front, my Plan B.

"There's a letter in there for you," I said. I handed you the envelope. "There's also a list of my favorite movies. If you watch them and you like them, if you ever change your mind, please come and find me."

I wobbled back to my car, threw mom's heels in the backseat and drove off. My parents thought I was at the lock-in, so I couldn't go home. I knew there was a Super 8 fifteen minutes away; I got on the highway and headed east. Once I was in the room, I turned on the TV, turned down the air conditioner as far as it would go and stripped off my clothes. This time, I just pulled the covers over my head and listened to the muffled voice of a news anchor talking about a drug bust from earlier in the evening.

Do you want to know about my life since that night, Officer Birch? Well, you don't get to. Not now, maybe never. You can make up something if you'd like. Make me a good girl, make me a responsible adult. Make me a slut. I really don't care.

Twelve years. You finally came and found me. How did you track me down? If you called my parents, I'm sure they hung up on you. I guess the *how* doesn't really matter. You got my email address, and you sent a one-line message with an attachment.

The message said, "Do you still feel this way?"

The attachment was a scanned picture of the letter from graduation night. Some of the ink was smudged, and the paper had deep creases, as if it had been folded and unfolded many times.

I should've lied. I should've said how happy I was. I could have made up a wonderful wife and six or seven children, a family of love and a marriage of lust.

I should've lied, but I didn't. I just typed, "Yes," and hit REPLY.

You sent me an address in our hometown, a date and a time.

I don't like to wear dresses, Officer Birch, but I dug out a low-cut red one for you. I found some heels. I got a haircut. And I made the long drive home all done up. I didn't stop to see my parents; there's no reason to go to a place where I'm not welcome. I just headed through town and out into the country. I had a map spread out on the front seat and managed to find the correct gravel road after a couple of wrong turns.

When I was close to the address, I heard the siren and saw the police car trailing me. I pulled over, got out and leaned against the door. When I saw you walking toward me, I was amazed at how good you looked. I was happy that the stress of being a cop hadn't aged you prematurely.

I didn't know what greeting would be appropriate. A hug didn't seem quite right. A handshake, maybe, would be better. When you reached me, you grabbed me and bent me over the hood of my car. You had me in handcuffs before I had a chance to say anything. Being cuffed with my hands behind me was not comfortable, and the metal dug in my skin when you dragged me to your car, my heels digging two jagged lines in the dirt and rocks.

You threw me in the backseat. It was difficult to see you through the wire mesh that divided the cops and the criminals.

"What took you so fucking long?" I said. "Twelve years? You made me wait twelve years before finding me?"

It looked like your shoulders slumped.

"I know," you said. "I'm sorry. I'm so sorry."

"Do you know what my life has been like, how lonely I've been? I've been dying for someone to come and take me away."

"It hasn't been easy for me either," you said, and I heard you sigh. "Are you with anyone?"

"That's none of your business. I'm here, aren't I?"

You pulled the car onto a bumpy side road. We went for at least a mile, and then you stopped the car and pulled me out. You led me into the woods. Branches slapped my face, and something thorny scratched my arm. We ended up at a small clearing, a square of dirt surrounded by four logs cut from very wide trees. You undid my cuffs, and I sat down on one of the logs, not caring if the bark ripped up my dress. You sat down on the other side of the square.

I knew this was your attempt to give me what I wanted. From the way you set up the entire encounter, I could tell you had watched the tapes. You were planning something similar, but I wasn't going to do anything until you answered my question.

"Did you know why I was at your door?" I said. "Before I gave you the letter. Did you know?"

"I don't want to talk about that right now."

"You don't want to talk about it?"

I should explain that the reason I yelled, "You fucking asshole!" and started toward you was to punch you in the face. I have never punched anyone before, but I was ready. You didn't want to talk about the defining moment of my life? You didn't want to give me any answers after waiting more than a decade to find me? How selfish, how awful a person could you be?

I made it halfway across the square. My right hand was balled into a fist, but then I looked at you. At your face, fighting back tears but not succeeding, your hand holding a folded-up piece of paper that could only be my letter.

I looked at your badge, still shiny. Your uniform, still spotless. The model cop. The perfect school resource officer. The woman who saved me from being bullied.

The cop who would never, ever let herself be attracted to a student, even if the student was a legal adult. The cop who would never give in, no matter what.

The woman who still wondered, even though so much time had passed, even though we were only a few years apart in age, if what she felt was wrong.

I dropped my fist and went to you. I removed your cap to find a perfectly formed flattop, sides and back shaved to the skin. I kneeled on the ground, grabbed your cheeks and I kissed you. On graduation night, I was certain our first kiss would be rough, maybe painful. This was a gentle kiss, sweet, not angry. I put my anger aside for the rest of that afternoon.

"I can't, I can't be like you want, not right now, not today," you said. "I had it all planned out so well. I can be hard, I promise, just like the videos, but..."

"Get up," I said.

You stood. I traced my index finger up and down your zipper and around the outline of the dick you packed especially for me. I pulled down the zipper, and I pulled your cock out through the hole in your men's briefs.

Your dick was so wonderful in my mouth, Officer Birch. It was warm, and my spit made it slippery so that it slid through my lips with ease. Your hands touched my head, guiding me to blow you the way you liked. Your mouth made a noise that was a cross between a moan and a growl.

With my index finger, I found my way behind the harness to your pussy. I knew that touching it might offend you. It had offended some of my butch lovers in the past. That day, I did it anyway. I rubbed your clit with my finger in a circular motion, then rubbed it between my finger and thumb. Every time I added pressure, you shuddered. When I took your dick out of my mouth and concentrated on you, putting the tips of my fingers inside your pussy, you shuddered even more.

But that wasn't what I wanted. I needed something else. I kicked off my shoes, pulled my dress over my head and literally ripped off my panties.

"Fuck me," I said. "Right now."

You were on top of me immediately. You kissed my mouth, my neck, and you nibbled on both ears. Then, you stuck your cock inside of me. You moved your hips in just the right way, putting it all the way in and then pulling it out so just the tip was inside.

You were fully clothed, and I loved that your body was still a mystery. Your badge cut me on my left breast; there's a sharp point somewhere on the shield that cut me and kept digging into me, but you didn't notice. The more it cut me, the more I wanted the pain. I wanted to bleed out everything inside of me and replace it with that feeling.

Right when I was about to come, you pulled out and rolled me over in the dirt.

"Get on all fours," you said. "Ass in the air."

That's what I had been waiting for all this time, Officer Birch. I did as I was told. I was scared, but I was so proud that I was able to take your entire cock inside my asshole. You didn't have to nudge it in. I took the whole thing right away.

You started growling loudly, and I felt like I was floating. I reached down and rubbed my clit. You pounded me so many times, more than I ever imagined I could take.

When I came, I screamed. You went on for a couple of seconds, but then you stopped, and I collapsed. Dirt got in my fingernails, in my mouth and ears, in my pussy. I rolled around on the ground because I was still coming down. I ended up caked in dirt.

You stood over me and grinned. You unbuckled your belt, and you maneuvered your dick through your pants as you took them off. You removed your underwear, your uniform top, your undershirt and your sports bra. Finally, you removed your dick.

"This is me," you said. "This is all of me."

Your arms were so muscular, your legs and your pussy so hairy. You looked like a sculpture, the perfect body carved out of wood.

I pounced on you. I wanted to devour you. I didn't have a strap-on, but I had fingers and a tongue and toes. You let me fuck you even though my body was filthy. You let me give you pleasure, and you came quickly, a lot quicker than I did. I felt bad that I couldn't make it last longer.

Or, is it something else? Do you allow yourself pleasure, Officer Birch? I'm not talking about masturbation or sex. I'm talking about letting down your guard for actual pleasure, for true desire. I don't let my guard down either, at least not very often. It's nothing to be ashamed of. You looked ashamed after your orgasm, after you squirted on the ground, making a small mark of mud. But, it's okay, Officer Birch. It really is.

"I'm sorry," you said. "I wanted to give you…"

"Shut up," I said. I kissed you, and I let you hold me, but I really didn't want a lecture. I think we're past that now.

* * *

So here we are, Officer Birch. Was this a one-time thing? The start of something everlasting? Will I ever see you again? I've given you my address and phone number. You haven't moved so I know where you live.

Can we build something out of this, or should this be the end of the story? I don't know. I'm not sure if I should make the next move, or if it's your turn. I'm still not very good at this.

There is one final thing I think I should share with you. Actually, I want to share it with you. It was scary and sad at the time, but it happened and it's part of my life. Maybe sharing will help us answer these questions.

This is an excerpt from my journal, from after my junior year of college when I was home for the summer:

> *I forgot to close the lock on my fire safe. Mom found all of it, the old VHS tapes and the new DVD that shipped right before I moved back.*
>
> *"Are you a dyke?" she asked me. I had just come home from work to find her sitting on my bed, crying, with porn sprawled all over the comforter.*
>
> *"Why are you going through my personal stuff?"*
>
> *"Just tell me, damn it. Are you a fucking dyke?"*
>
> *"Yes!" I screamed. "Couldn't you tell? Didn't you wonder why I've never had a real boyfriend? I'm not that ugly. Some girls up at school even like me."*
>
> *"Shut up," she said. "Just shut up. I'm so disgusted right now, I don't know what to think."*
>
> *"Are you going to kick me out? Make me leave, another gay runaway living on the streets?"*
>
> *She had stopped crying by this point, but she didn't answer my question. "These tapes..."*

"You don't bring up the tapes, and I won't ask what you and Dad are into, okay? You know Dad has porn. I know where he keeps it."

"What are we going to do?" she said. "Do people know? You can't tell anyone we know."

"I'm out at school. I know how to tell people, and I don't really care what they think. I definitely don't care if it embarrasses you." I said that last part just to be mean. I wish I hadn't said it.

"All right," she said, "I know you think you understand things. But a woman is not supposed to love another woman. Two women cannot actually be in love."

"You're wrong," I said. Now I started crying, but I kept talking, and my voice kept getting louder. "I do love another woman. I've been in love with Officer Birch for four years now. I love her so much it hurts. And I'll never, ever have her. I tried once, and I failed."

"It will pass," Mom said. "It was just a crush. In a while, you won't even remember her name."

"It won't pass," I said. I dried my eyes, and I looked directly at my mother. "My love for her will never go away. I wish it would. I've tried to make it stop, but I can't. I just can't do it. I need her."

RAVEN BRINGS THE LIGHT

Kenzie Mathews

Thomasane didn't want to talk about it when she finally came home, but I'd been watching the news. I find monotones soothing when grading the kids' papers. I like white noise in the background while I think. According to the news report, the body found in the abandoned Toyota Corolla had been identified as Libby Shields. I stopped grading the minute the newscaster said her name.

I remembered the girl: pretty, thin, elfishly punk with her facial piercings. She'd come to my class a few times to pick up her younger brother's art homework. Once, she'd asked me about Van Gogh. Why was he so important now, when in his time, he'd been a freak? I don't remember now what I said, but it made her smile. Sad, soft, fleeting.

I watched the news now, thinking of that smile.

Last October, twenty-year-old Libby Shields left her house with just the clothes on her back. Her mother thought she might come home once Libby realized she'd left behind her purse and driver's license. They'd argued before and Libby always came back once she cooled off. The night turned into weeks, and then months. And then it was April with the snow and ice breaking up under the weight of long fierce sunlight.

Come breakup, everything hidden rises up.

A man jogging on the highway followed his dog to an abandoned car. The Labrador went crazy, pawing wildly at the window on the passenger side. The jogger came closer when the smell overwhelmed him. Sweet as old perfume, thick as smoke, it made him choke and gag. Covering his mouth and nose with his elbow, he peered in. At first he thought the car had to be filled with rotten fish or rancid moose roadkill. But the slight shape hidden beneath a gray military parka was too big to be an ice chest of fish, too small to be moose. His dog knew already and barked nonstop.

The jogger called the troopers on his cell, occasionally waving his arms at the passing cars. It was ironic in a way; the highway was always busy as it connected several small communities to a major city. Even in the dead of winter, the highway was heavily policed and populated. And yet, here Libby was, hidden in a Toyota Corolla, buried by snow for six months.

The only thing Alaska promises for sure is a beautiful death.

Thomasane and her partner Brady were the first Troopers on scene. And I know that it's not because Thomasane is some super trooper, *even though she is*...it's just that it's all small-town out here. We're such a small collection of communities, we only have four pairs of Troopers. But the territory they cover is vast.

So, now when Thomasane said instead, "Chris, did I ever tell you about Raven and the Hunters?" I said no, even though I'm pretty sure I told her that story first.

I put down my graded papers, pushing the dogs off the couch

to make room for Thomasane. They settled on the floor, one on each side of me. My Chow Shepherd mix, Raulie, sat on my left. Ginger, the Labrador Rottweiler mix, lay down next to my right side.

Thomasane unbuckled her gun belt and hung it on the coatrack next to the front door. She covered it with her brown Alaska State Trooper jacket. I patted the couch beside me and gave her my best and campiest come-hither look; I'm terrible at flirting, but I cover my inadequacies with self-mocking overexaggeration. Thomasane said once when we were first dating that clowns were holy. That's funny to me, because I think clowns are terrifying. What are they really thinking behind the makeup and costumes?

Either way, Thomasane thinks I'm funny. I guess it all works out in the end. In Thomasane's family, no one ever dared to laugh or smile, much less talk. Even now, when her family calls, I know who it is based on the silence and breathing at the other end of the phone. Thomasane's half Russian, a quarter Norwegian, and a quarter Native. She's tall, dark and muscular, her blue-black shoulder length hair always pulled back tight in a ponytail, her black eyes unreadable.

In my family, all we did was laugh, even when the joke hurt. It stopped us from killing each other or committing suicide. I'm all Irish: short with curves and pale, with embarrassingly uncontrollable reddish brown hair.

Thomasane lay down next to me, her feet up on the couch and her head in my lap. I stroked her face, my hands cupping her chin and throat, feeling the tightness there loosen, feeling her swallow slowly, counting the slowing pulse in her neck.

Thomasane said, "Raven was eating on the beach and a hunter came up to him. 'I'm hungry,' said the hunter. 'Do you know where the good meat is?'

"Raven peered at him, thinking. Finally, Raven said, 'See that island across the ocean? See that cave? All the hunters say it's good hunting there.'

"So the hunter made a kayak out of his spears and parka. He was cold but he was hungry more. Then, the hunter took his kayak out into the ocean to row to the island. Raven flew above him, still chewing his meal. The hunter climbed out of his kayak and walked to the cave entrance.

"He peered into the darkness of the cave and asked Raven, 'Where is the meat, Raven?' Raven knocked the heavy stones down from the top of the cave onto the hunter's head, killing the hunter instantly.

"'You're the meat, stupid,' Raven said, eating the hunter's face. 'I just don't know why they fall for that every time.'"

"Oh, honey," I said to Thomasane, kissing her soft mouth, my hand still cupping her chin.

My mouth lingered over hers and softly, she kissed me back, her tongue stroking, licking at my mouth. My other hand slid into her uniform and underneath her bra until it cupped her breast; her nipple hardened in my palm. I pulled and rolled her nipple between my knuckles, not quite cruel but close enough.

Thomasane rose and climbed fully on top of me. I lifted my hips when she unzipped my jeans and pulled my damp panties off, curling my legs alongside her hips, my sex open to her fingers. I bucked into her; her fingers opened like a flower inside me. We fucked, her thumb circling round and round on my clit, her hand curling and unraveling in my cunt, her tongue deep in my mouth. I howled into her mouth when I came.

Afterward, lying in the tangle of our limbs, I reached out to stroke her through her brown pants, to return the favor. Thomasane shook her head, no, and rose off the couch. "Can't," she mumbled at me, "Have to take a shower. Going back to work.

Brady can't handle all the paperwork."

I listened to the shower turn on. I sat up, found my panties and put them on. I got my jeans midway up my calves and then just stopped and kicked them back off again. I looked at the kids' paperwork and, despite myself, even though I thought I was going to just breathe and keep it all under wraps, I kicked at the artwork savagely. Pages of water-colored landscapes flew in the air.

The dogs looked at me, eyes wide. Ginger got up and moved away from me, feeling the waves of my anger. I'd rescued her from abuse at an early age. Raulie stayed close, unwilling to let me suffer alone. I'd gotten him from a feral street litter. They each dealt with humans based on their own past. They'd both come a long way toward healing and, in turn, often healed me.

I felt like laughing. It was a lot like my relationship with Thomasane. It all came back to her crappy violent childhood, trying to protect her younger siblings from her alkie dad and weak, druggy mom. What was it Thomasane said when she thought I was cutting too close with the questions? Oh, yeah. *I'm not one of your dogs, Chris. You can't save me.* Really? I wasn't the only one. What about her need to protect everyone else?

I buried my face in my hands, too angry to cry but my eyes burning so badly that the light was killing me. Ginger came, pressing her back into my legs. I petted her absently, worrying already. Yes, Thomasane was going to go back to work to help finish up the paperwork that Brady could never do alone. Then, they'd go to a bar and drink. They'd drink and not talk, come home and not talk some more.

I snorted up bitter sharp laughter. Maybe I should call Karen, Brady's wife, and together we could start a Cop Wives Support Group. I even had a tagline for the group: "Women who love ticking-bomb cops who drink too much, collect guns and never share their pain."

I knelt down and gently collected the kids' artwork. I soothed the wrinkles, worried at a few tears in the pages. Finding my breath again, I concentrated on grading and grading alone. Line, shadow, space, composition, color choices, originality. When Thomasane came out of the bathroom, smelling of Lever 2000 and lavender shampoo, I stared at her, silently demanding that she acknowledge me. She came to me and kissed the side of my mouth harshly, possessively, before walking out the front door.

By the time Thomasane came home, the house smelled thickly of grilled garlic steak, onions and mashed potatoes. I'd made a hot green-bean salad with almond slices, baked honeyed corn muffins, and tossed up an imitation crab salad with cherry tomatoes and tofu. Dessert was Thomasane's favorite: cherry pie à la mode. I'd set the table up with the food and lit fat, smoky, vanilla musk candles.

All of these delicious smells barely covered the smell of sweaty, spoiled, happily-run-to-bone-weary-sleep dogs, though. So, I'd lit sandalwood incense and sprayed the carpet, chairs, couch, Raulie and Ginger with extra strength Febreze. Then I'd locked Raulie and Ginger up in our bedroom.

I think it helped that I was also completely nude except for high heels and a string of pearls. I didn't want to fight anymore. I wanted to feel her inside me. I just wanted to fuck and not think about anything else. Ever again.

Thomasane was happily, almost gratefully surprised. She sat down at the table, forgetting to remove her gun belt and jacket. She looked at me and grinned, which was hard for her to do. Before me, I doubt seriously she'd ever even smiled.

"Loocy," Thomasane said in a kick-ass Desi Arnaz imitation, "I think you have some esplanning to do."

I knelt down next to her and gently removed her gun belt. Then I climbed onto her lap, facing her, the edge of the dinner table digging into my back. I bounced a little, my nipples digging into her brown uniform, my cunt already warm and wet on her lap, my arms wrapped around her neck. "Ooh, T, can't that wait until after we eat?"

Laughing a little, Thomasane reached around me and cut a piece of steak. She swirled it slowly in the A.1. sauce and brought it back, dripping, over my shoulder. Softly, she dabbed my collarbones with the steak and sauce. Sauce dribbled down my breasts. Then, she fed me the steak while she sucked and licked at my chest, lifting me nearly onto the table to suckle a nipple. I moaned, my legs grasping her waist tightly.

Thomasane lifted me fully onto the table, and I pushed her plate out of the way. One by one, she lined my stomach with warm green beans and almonds. I giggled, my hands in Thomasane's slick black hair, cradling her head. Thomasane sucked the bean juice out of my belly button, her tongue teasing flickers there that I felt all the way to my cunt. I ground against her, my hips rising. Thomasane stroked my swelling labia lips, tickling me with the barest of fingertips. I ground against her fingers, her now-slick palm.

Reaching behind me, I found the mashed potatoes. I smeared a handful into Thomasane's mouth, both of us laughing, and then I rose up, pulling her back down with me as my tongue and fingers explored her mouth hungrily. I opened her brown shirt, shoving her white bra out of my way. I nibbled on her breasts, sucked hard and chewed lightly on her long hard nipples.

Thomasane continued to stroke my wet snatch until, anxious for her, I shoved her hand inside me. I gasped, not really ready for her entire hand but so desperate for her, needing her so much that I couldn't wait. Thomasane closed her hand so not to hurt me and I calmed, relaxed, taking her. I trusted her completely. I wished she felt the same about me. Thomasane kissed me hard and long, demandingly, possessively as we slowly fucked.

Around midnight, a sixty-nine-year-old man called 911 and confessed to the murder of Libby Shields. It was just a stupid accident, he said. He hadn't meant to do it. The Emergency Operator asked if he wanted to turn himself in. The man was silent for a moment. Finally, he said he guessed so. The Operator asked if he needed a police escort and then asked calmly for directions to his whereabouts. He gave them to her, his voice cracking midway through. The Operator sent the information into the station.

The phone woke me but Thomasane was faster, reaching over me to catch it. By her sudden stillness, I knew what it was, who it was even before she explained in a rush. She dressed quickly in silence, to the soft red light of her bedside lamp. When she leaned over to kiss me, it was hurried and wet. Her side of the bed was still warm when I heard her truck leave.

I sat there in the soft red-lit room, unable to sleep now that she was gone. When Raulie and Ginger poked their heads around the bedroom doorframe, I clicked my tongue to the roof of my mouth, calling them in. I let them settle in Thomasane's spot and cuddled close to them. Even though I closed my eyes, sleep still eluded me.

When it was almost a decent hour, I got up and dressed, leaving the dogs to sleep on the bed. I sucked down coffee quickly and shoveled peanut butter toast into my mouth. Thomasane hadn't called me since leaving at midnight to go pick up the man who'd confessed to Libby Shields's murder. It had me a little worried. She always found time to call me. Slowing down from 90 to 35,

I pulled into town. My old truck nearly sighed in relief. Thomasane and Brady weren't at the station. I went over to sit next to Thomasane's desk.

Absently, Trooper Harding called out, "She's not coming back any time soon."

I looked at him.

"She and Brady are at the hospital. Brady nearly got his foot cut off with a machete." Blood drained from my face. Harding went on, "Thomasane's okay. She shot the perp."

Karen beat me to the hospital, but then I guess if it'd been Thomasane with a machete-chopped foot, I'd have moved heaven and earth also. I stood next to Thomasane while they gave Brady more drugs. His foot was wrapped up and held in a sling. Karen couldn't stop crying. I reached out and held Thomasane's hand. After a few minutes, she squeezed back.

"They say he'll keep his toes and his nerves aren't severed," Karen said with brave melodrama, crying still. "But there'll be a scar."

I said very seriously, keeping a straight face, "Nothing could be worse." Thomasane squeezed my hand in warning. Not everyone enjoys dark Irish humor.

Brady shook his head in disgust. "Bastard threw a machete at me." He looked at me bleary-eyed. "A machete. Why not an axe? What's wrong with an axe?"

"You should go home," Thomasane whispered into my ear, "I still have to get my full confession."

I stared wide-eyed at her. I whispered, "He's here?"

Thomasane smiled at me, laughing at my reaction. "I'm a damn fine shot. He's just wounded. He'll live to serve time for Libby's death."

"Are you in trouble for shooting him?"

"Self-defense." She motioned toward Brady. The drugs were kicking in. Brady was examining the fat fleshy knot his hand made wrapped within Karen's. Thomasane went on, "Brady's my witness. The perp threw a weapon at both of us during the middle of the interview."

I nodded. Thomasane led me out of Brady's room and into the hallway. For a moment, she held my hand in both of hers and then, she let it fall away. It's a small town after all. Small-town judgment. Head down, I snorted in bitter laughter. I turned away.

"Chris," Thomasane called softly after me. I kept walking but then, my pride and anger and fear just died within me. I only felt gratitude. Thomasane was alive. Brady would heal. And Libby Shields's murderer would face justice for his crime. In the bigger picture of it all, it was petty of me to cling to small annoyances. I turned back around to face Thomasane. Smiling gently, I said, "I'll be waiting for you at home."

When Thomasane got home, I had a hot bath waiting. I'd started drawing and draining the bath hours before. I hadn't known it would take her so long to get home to me. But I guess, with Brady in the hospital on medical leave, all the paperwork was hers to do. When she let me undress her, I knew she'd done all the drinking for both of them, too.

She sighed once in the tub, the steam rising up to fog the mirrors. I bathed her and scrubbed her gently with lavender-scented bath soap. Thomasane hates scented bath oils. That's how I knew for sure that she was more intoxicated than usual. It was on the tip of my tongue to mention to her that it'd be a tragedy if she were to get a DUI right after shooting a perp, but this softness, this unusual vulnerability in her stopped me.

I said instead, "I'm glad it was Brady instead of you."

Thomasane's eyes popped open, her body tensing, but she didn't say anything for a while. Then, when I thought she was going to keep it all inside, like always: "It's always something stupid like that. Something you wouldn't think could happen. Stupid evil is what gets you in the end. True evil you can fight. It's noble, you can see it. You can find justice for true evil, but stupid evil? You die a joke."

I didn't know what to say to that, how to answer to that. So, instead, I said, "Hey, T, did I ever tell you about when Raven brought the light?"

"No," Thomasane said, closing her eyes again, even though she knew the story better than I did. "How did Raven bring the light?"

I bathed her as I spoke, her limbs drowsy and liquid in my hands. "Once," I said, kissing her neck, "the world was wrapped in darkness because the Sky Chief kept the sun, moon and the stars in boxes in his house. To keep the light safe, the Sky Chief never let it out. Everyone in the world, however, stumbled in darkness, afraid and hungry, violent and stupid, praying for light. Raven watched this and grew bored. So he turned himself into a tiny black seed and threw himself into a drinking well. Along came the Sky Chief's beautiful daughter. Thirsty, she drank from the well, swallowing the black seed that was Raven."

I soaped Thomasane's breasts, her brown areoles wrinkling as her nipples stirred. I leaned down and kissed each one. Thomasane purred in her throat, smiling. I licked one nipple and sucked at the other. I kissed her mouth solidly, quickly, before rising up again to tell the story. Thomasane draped one wet hand over my thigh. I lifted and soaped her thigh, while my fingers traced circles and waves like disappearing tattoos on her inner thighs.

I continued, "The Sky Chief's beautiful daughter became pregnant with the seed that was Raven. She gave birth to a beautiful little boy who carried Raven's soul inside him. The Sky Chief was so pleased with his grandson, he spoiled him rotten. Then, on the child's third birthday, the Sky Chief asked him what he wanted for his three birthday gifts."

I moved to the side of the tub to start washing Thomasane's other leg. Her eyes still closed, she rose slightly out of the tub to give me a kiss; her wet breasts dampened my shirt, stirring me. My own nipples rose in answer and fire, and longing shot downward to my groin. When she released me, I pulled my damp shirt over my head and threw it behind me. Thomasane laughed a little, and her fingers danced delicately over the raised nipple in my bra.

"What did the Raven child want?" Her black unreadable eyes twinkled.

I smiled and answered, "He wanted the moon, the sun and the stars that the Sky Chief kept in boxes. The Sky Chief loved his grandson, even if Raven was his soul, and so he gave the boxes to the child. And once the boxes were in his hands, Raven released himself from the body cage and flew upward, stealing the moon, the sun and the stars away. Then, there in the sky, Raven threw the stars as far as he could so that they could reach all the dark parts of the earth. The people below screamed in delight. Raven released the moon, and she ran to the far corner of the sky so she could shine shyly like a maiden. The people below jumped up and down, clapping their hands. Then, Raven tossed up the golden ball sun so that it ran across the sky happily like a child in fields. The people danced in happiness, overcome with the light in their lives. Now, the people knew that even when everything seems overwhelmed with evil, good is coming. It is just that sometimes it is the dark itself that brings the light."

I finished washing Thomasane's other leg and slowly put it back into the warm water. Thomasane took my hand and guided it to her cunt. I washed her slowly, completely, soaping her nether lips, circling her clit with my thumb. When she was clean to my satisfaction, I stroked her, my fingers fucking her slowly, playfully. I drained the tub with my other hand.

Trembling, relying entirely on me, Thomasane stepped out of the tub. I knelt before her, looked up at her and kissed her cunt until she spread her legs and let me in.

HEALING HAND

Lynn Mixon

Normal people didn't reach for a shotgun when an unexpected visitor pulled into their driveway. I hadn't been normal for a long time, so as soon as I heard the crunch of gravel, I grabbed my 12-gauge and peeked through the drapes.

The sleek black SUV pulling up to my gate confirmed my suspicions. None of my neighbors owned anything that fancy, and they knew better than to just drop in.

A shotgun is a handy thing. You hardly ever have to use it, but in some situations, nothing else will cut it. Snakes and strangers, for example. You never quite knew exactly what either would do.

Turned out, after all, I knew the tall, blonde woman in the beat-up bomber jacket who climbed out of the SUV. Five years wasn't nearly long enough to forget someone like US Marshal Lily Callahan. My chest tightened a little at the memories the sight of her brought up.

She'd shepherded me through testifying at trial and entering the witness protection program five years ago. While she hadn't done anything obvious, I knew she was attracted to me. The fascination had been mutual, though it took me a while to understand why. I'd had a thing for bad boys for most of my life, and her tough-as-nails cop attitude pushed those same buttons. I'd thought many times about how things might have been different if I'd followed through on those feelings, but I'd bluffed myself out of that hand.

I sighed and let the drape fall. She wasn't here to talk about old times. Whatever had brought her up into the mountains couldn't be good.

I opened the door just as she raised her hand to knock. Up close, she looked thinner and more worn than I remembered, more haggard. We stood staring at one another for a moment before she spoke.

"That's a nice shotgun you have there," she said. "I didn't piss you off the last time we talked, did I?"

I allowed my lips to quirk. "Nothing personal. We mountain folk keep them around to deal with critters and revenuers."

The corners of her mouth inched up. "While I *am* a federal agent, I'm not with the Treasury Department." Her gaze took a slow trip down to my feet and back to my face. She definitely still found me attractive. "You look good, Maverick."

I hadn't heard that nickname in a long time. It was a nod to Bret Maverick, the gambler from the most awesome TV show ever. It reminded me of the life I'd had to walk away from, and it hurt like hell hearing her say it.

"I'm Leann Parker these days, at least according to the birth certificate your people conjured up for me."

She took off her shades and slipped them into her jacket, looking at her scuffed boots as she toed the ground. The skin under her eyes was dark, and her face was gray. Sleep, it appeared, wasn't among her top priorities. Guilt tinged her voice, though I couldn't tell if it was for checking me out or reminding me of my lost past. "Yeah...I shouldn't have brought that up. Sorry."

"I think you better come on in and tell me what's on your mind. You didn't drive all the way up here for nothing." I glanced past her at the SUV. There weren't any other people with her. I stepped back and opened the door wide. "Where's that clean-cut partner of yours?"

She didn't answer right away. Instead, she walked past me to the window where I'd stood earlier and stared out. "He's in the hospital," she said softly.

I closed the door, set the shotgun against the easy chair and walked up behind her. She flinched a bit when I laid my hand on her shoulder. "I'm sorry to hear that. What happened?"

Lily reached up and covered my hand with hers. It was rough and calloused, like mine. Standing this close, her apple-scented shampoo flooded my senses. The firmness of her muscular shoulder under the soft leather of her jacket made my heart beat a little faster.

She half-turned toward me. I knew my expression showed no sign of how she affected me. I hadn't gambled professionally for five long years, but my poker face was still in place.

Anger and guilt fought for control in her eyes. "Jake Latrell escaped from prison last week. He almost killed Karl, and he's looking for you."

My stomach did a slow, queasy roll. I'd been afraid of something like this ever since I'd testified against the mob boss. A blast of cold adrenaline shot through me, and I took a sharp breath. "Oh, my god! I need to get out of here."

She grabbed my arm as I started toward the shotgun. "He's not going to find you here. Trust me, I'll keep you safe."

I forced myself to stand still, but I could feel my face twitching.

Even *my* control wasn't good enough to block outright terror. Latrell had killed a man right in front of me, and I had no doubt he'd be happy to do the same *to* me.

Lily wrapped her arms around me, anger and despair replaced by the same comforting demeanor she'd used to keep me sane before the trial. I didn't know how she could do it, putting her own pain on the back burner while dealing with mine.

Her warmth sank into me, and her closeness muted my fear to manageable levels. I brought my trembling hands to her hips, buried my face in her hair and cried. The hot tears humiliated me, but once they started, I couldn't stop them.

She whispered soft words in my ear and stroked my hair until I finally raised my head and wiped at my face. My body chose that moment to react to her pressing against me. Tingles ran across my skin, tightening my breasts and making my breath catch a bit in my throat.

Lily's face turned a nice shade of pink. She felt it, too. The attraction was still there, but, again, the timing sucked. I slowly pulled away from our embrace.

"I need some tea before I can wrap my head around this," I said. "Please, have a seat."

"Sounds great," she said, with a hint of regret in her voice. Relief, too, unless I missed my guess. Our mutual sexual awareness put her in an ethical quandary. She wanted me, but she was responsible for me.

I left her eyeing the furniture scattered around my living room and walked into the kitchen. With practiced motions, I lit the gas stove and quickly had a kettle of water heating while my thoughts raced. I had no idea what to do about Latrell—or Lily.

The ritual of boiling water and setting up for tea calmed me. By the time I walked back into the living room I had regained my composure.

She'd settled on the love seat. Good call. The couch had a spring that would change the religion of the unwary.

I sat next to her. "Thank you for the hug. I really needed it."

Her lips curved upward. "It was my pleasure."

It had been mine, too. "Okay, first things first. Is Karl going to be okay?"

Her expression darkened. "He'll live, but it's going to be a long recovery. Latrell and his goons really hurt him. They broke both arms, both legs, smashed his hands and snapped eight ribs. They left him for dead, but he still managed to call 911."

I touched her arm for a moment. "That's horrible. I understand why Latrell wants me dead. You don't cross the likes of him and just walk away. But why attack Karl? You guys didn't arrest him."

She shrugged, her fingers nervously tapping on her leg. "I expect he thought we could access some government database and find your new identity. When he found out we couldn't, he had his men beat Karl with a tire iron."

I looked down, suddenly aware of how bad off Karl really was. "I'm so sorry."

Her flat voice did nothing to hide her pain. I ached, watching her struggle to keep her tears back. "Latrell tore up my apartment first, but I wasn't there. If I'd been home, Karl might be okay."

"Then you'd have been beaten, maybe killed." Just the thought of her being hurt squeezed my heart.

"I'd rather it had happened to me." Lily leaned back on the love seat, sorrow etching her beautiful face. "He'll never fully recover. He's got a wife and kids, for God's sake."

"He's alive. You have to focus on that. What else can you do?"

She sat up, her eyes blazing. "I want to track the son of a

bitch down and empty my clip into him, then reload so I can do it all again. But they won't let me. They wouldn't even let me stay with Karl." The pain in her voice bled through her rage.

I wanted to tell her I'd help reload, but that wasn't helpful. Instead, I took her hand into mine. "Your boss made the right decision. I know you're hurting, but you have to trust that they'll catch up with him and make him pay. I seem to remember you telling me that very same thing the last time we were together."

Her lips twisted. "Trusting the system doesn't seem to have worked out so well for any of us where that bastard Latrell is concerned."

I nodded. "Yeah. You said he wouldn't find me here. Is that true?"

"If he had any real chance of finding you, they would've sent a van full of marshals to hustle you off to a safe house. My presence here is insurance, nothing more."

I opened my mouth to tell her she was hardly just that, but she cut me off. "I really can't talk about this right now." She took a deep breath and looked around. "You have a nice place here, and it looks like you've settled in pretty well. Found a good-looking guy to heat up your nights?"

"Out here?" I choked. "You've got to be kidding. The men around here think a good time involves beer, monster trucks and country music." I shuddered. "I can't stand country music."

She shook her head and smiled. "I'm sure you could convince someone to turn the radio off once in a while."

"Maybe, but I never found anyone worth the headache. I still have big-city tastes, and while I'm sure the men here are as good as anywhere else, they just don't interest me. I'll stick with silicone, thanks."

The sharp whistle of the kettle cut off whatever response she was going to make and gave me an excuse to focus my attention elsewhere while I considered what to say next. Not that it helped, because I was still thinking when I came back with our chamomile tea. She took hers and immediately set it down on the coffee table.

I sat beside her, sipped the soothing liquid and watched her over the rim of my cup. She'd rebuilt her "tough cop" façade, smoothing over the cracks of weakness she'd shown. Her life revolved around protecting others: comforting them through the pain and chaos of entering the witness protection program and leaving everyone and everything they had ever known behind them. In the time I'd spent with her before, I'd never heard her sound like she needed help and healing in her own life.

Whether she admitted it or not, she did now, and I wanted to be the one to help her.

"I like it here well enough," I said. "The quiet relaxes me, but I miss playing cards. None of my neighbors will play with me anymore, not after an unfortunate incident at the county fair."

That sounded pretty, but it was bullshit. I hated living way out here, hiding from men who wanted me dead. Every single day I fought the urge to drive to Vegas, find a high-stakes game and play until the men with no necks came to drag me to my death. I missed that life so badly I could taste it.

The corner of Lily's mouth twitched. "Liar. Don't try to fool a cop. Me, I'd love to live out here. These days, it seems like the only time I get to explore the great outdoors is when I'm on a manhunt. The rest of my time is spent babysitting witnesses."

That brought a smile to my face. "It wasn't Disneyland, but looking back it wasn't so bad."

She sniffed. "Maybe from your perspective. I seem to recall losing six months' pay at the poker table."

"I forgave that and the fifteen years' pay the other marshals owed me. I even gave back that one guy's Harley."

"How generous." Her shoulders relaxed a little. "There were some good things about being locked in a cabin with you, though."

I made a mental note to thank god for that opening next Sunday. "Like what?"

Lily shrugged. "You have a wonderful personality, and it was great watching you beat the pants off Paul Jenkins, the jerk. Being with you didn't feel like work at all. It was more like summer camp."

"Lily, you lived in my back pocket for three weeks straight. I don't think you took a minute off. You should get away and have a real vacation." I took another sip of my tea. "You're always so focused on everyone else that you never take time to heal your own wounds. You need to smell the flowers and get laid before you go bonkers."

Her eyes widened. "I know the woman with no love life isn't telling me I need to do the horizontal mambo."

"Maybe I am." I hadn't realized it, but I'd just made the first move in this dance. The time was right to raise the stakes.

She laughed bitterly. "I can't just turn the job off. I don't get to have a personal life. When I am at home—which is rarely—all I do is think about work. And don't get me started on dating. Either my badge turns them off, or their parole officer calls while we're making out."

I shook my head slowly, smiling at her bad joke. "You over-think things. Sometimes you just need to take a chance. I learned that playing poker."

"All I know about poker is to fold when the cards suck."

"People fold too often when they shouldn't. Sometimes you have to go big even if you don't know how the hand is going to play out." I set my teacup on the saucer beside hers, pushed aside the butterflies in my stomach and kissed her. That hollow place inside me that I had suppressed for so long opened up and desire raced through me.

She stiffened and pushed me back. "What are you doing?"

"Something I should've done five years ago. Back then, I was too lost in my own fear to see what was right in front of me. I'm not going to make that mistake again."

Her mouth opened and closed twice before she found the words to speak. "I think you misunderstood something."

"Did I? I don't think so." I smiled as I leaned in again, my nose almost touching hers. My nervousness had vanished, replaced by the confidence of a professional gambler who knew she held the winning hand. "You wanted me then, and you want me now. I can see it in your eyes."

And I could. The blooming arousal she protested didn't exist made her pupils grow larger as I watched, signaling the heat building inside her even better than the red flush that crept up her neck.

She licked her lips, a nervous habit I hadn't seen from her before. In gambling, we called that a "tell." "Look, I don't think either of us needs this kind of—"

Sometimes talking is a mistake. I captured her lips with mine again and, after a moment's hesitation, she melted against me. Her mouth opened in surrender to my advances, and she brought her hands to my arms. My heart soared.

Her wet mouth hinted at mint and honey and wasn't anything like I'd expected. I kissed her soft lips and stroked her tongue with mine while my heart pounded. Raw hunger deepened my urgency. I only remembered to breathe when my lungs started burning.

We broke apart enough for her to look into my eyes. The haunted look was gone, replaced by raging desire. "I thought you weren't interested in girls."

"I'm interested in you."

I pulled her jacket off her arms and eyed her shoulder holster. It held a big, black gun that looked intimidating just sitting there. I reached for the strap, but Lily stopped me and slid it off effortlessly. It made a dull thud as she set it on the coffee table.

Her hands slipped between us, squeezing my breasts. A bolt of heat flashed down my spine and straight to my pussy. In an instant, I went from moist to dripping wet. I wanted her like I'd never wanted anyone else.

"I wish I had tits like yours." Lily's nimble fingers went to work on my buttons. My pulse raced at her whisper. My already tight nipples contracted almost painfully.

She licked her lips again as soon as she exposed the upper swells of my tanned breasts, cradled in my pink cotton bra. This time she didn't look nervous at all. Her eyes reluctantly moved to my face. "We shouldn't be doing this, but I want you. I need you. I need...this."

I tangled my fingers in her thick, flaxen hair and pulled her face closer to my breasts. She took a deep breath and let it out slowly, raising gooseflesh on my cleavage. I closed my eyes, and emotions I couldn't even name chased each other through me, leaving me trembling.

Her soft kisses on my cotton-covered flesh felt extraordinary. My body flushed with heat, awakening at her touch. It spread across my chest, down into my stomach, and even lower. I shrugged out of my blouse with shaking hands and fumbled with the catch on the front of my bra. She took my globes into her hands as soon as they popped free, rubbing her thumbs across my nipples, making me gasp.

She ducked her head and captured one between her lips. Jolts of electric pleasure shot through me, and my skin became so sensitive that I could feel every strand of her hair as it gently brushed against me.

When I couldn't take it anymore, I pulled her up and started unbuttoning her blouse. I felt like a virgin rounding third base. She smiled indulgently at my clumsiness, not rushing me or trying to take over. When I finally slid my hands up her bare sides, she shuddered.

Her unassuming white bra completely covered her small, firm breasts, but not for long. It quickly joined the growing pile on the floor.

Her nipples were tiny, almost as small as a man's, but no one could mistake them for anything but all female. I smiled up at her bright eyes and bent my head to run the tip of my tongue around one hard nub.

"Oh, yes," she hissed through clenched teeth.

I cupped her breasts in my hands and massaged them. Being with Lily didn't feel nearly as strange as I'd expected. Just the idea of kissing my way between those muscular thighs made my heart flutter with anticipation.

She let me spend a few wonderful minutes returning her earlier favors with interest before she pushed me back onto the love seat and hovered over me. "I need to taste you," she said, her voice rough.

Now her hands were trembling. I raised my hips so that she could tug my pants down. Unfortunately for her rising urgency, they tangled around my boots, and it took twice as long to get them off as it should have—which was three times slower than she wanted. By the time she finally got them off, she was shaking.

I lifted one of her hands and brushed my lips across it. She closed her eyes for a moment and took a deep breath. "I don't know what's come over me. I'm usually so smooth. Now I can't seem to control myself."

"I'm flattered. Make love to me, Lily."

Her hands steadied as she pulled my panties down. They were white and didn't match my bra, but I don't think she cared. She held the scrap of fabric to her nose for a moment before she dropped it and knelt between my legs. Torturing me with only her fingertips, she ran them from my ankles to my thighs so softly it bordered on tickling and had my body twitching in seconds.

She seemed to know just when I couldn't take it anymore and planted her palms against my inner thighs. Her blue eyes twinkled mischievously at me. "Should I stop?"

"Don't you dare!"

She laughed, the first happy sound she had made since arriving at my door. "I am so going to enjoy this."

Slowly, tenderly, she kissed my mound. Her breath shot across my aching pussy like a hot desert wind, raising a whirlwind of sensation that swept around my body. I moaned and lifted my hips, seeking more contact. I needed her now.

She eased my lips apart and slipped first one finger, then another inside me. I arched my back and pushed against her as she caressed my most intimate places. Her lips and tongue never slowed, melting my core.

When she sucked my clit, I thought my brain would explode. Her nimble tongue danced across it while her lips coaxed it from its hood. Electricity hummed throughout my body as she devoured my pussy, thrusting those wonderful fingers deep inside me until the world vanished in an explosion of color and pleasure. I wasn't sure, but I may have even passed out.

When I could focus again, Lily was beside me smiling, kissing me softly and sweetly. At some point, she'd removed the rest of her clothes. "That was stunning," she whispered. "I can't tell you how good it makes me feel. Thank you."

I ran my fingers languidly across her cheek. "You sound like this is over. Far from it, my dear. It's my turn now."

"You know you don't have to do that."

"Oh, but I want to," I purred. And I did. More than I'd wanted anything in a long, long time. It was more than sexual need, too. I hungered to feel emotionally connected to someone again. I'd been incredibly lonely since leaving my past behind.

Her wide smile seemed like it might split her face in two. I stood on wobbly legs, and she took my place on the love seat, spreading her legs slightly. I could see the pink lips of her pussy through the damp blonde hair that covered her mound.

I settled to my knees and ran my hands along her firm calves. She had dancer's legs, long and lithe. Her smooth skin felt like silk against my hands. The scent of her aroused sex was intoxicating and I wanted to dive right in, but I forced myself to slow down. I wanted this to be perfect.

Starting at her ankles, I kissed my way to her knees, switching from leg to leg. Only when I was nibbling at her knee did I coax her legs apart far enough to start kissing my way between her thighs.

The flesh on her inner thighs was incredibly sensitive. Every lap of my tongue made her jump a little; when I took her between my teeth, she moaned. I was so lost in teasing her that I only realized I was at her center when her damp pubic hair brushed my cheek.

I closed my eyes and inhaled her fragrance. It made my mouth water and my heart race. I paused for one last moment, gazing at her beautiful sex, before I took that final step onto the wild side.

I kissed her soaked mound and opened my eyes to watch her while I performed this most intimate act. I wanted to savor the moment, because first times never come again. Her dew tasted like the juice I sometimes sucked off my own fingers during what passed for sex out here alone, but there were subtle differences. She tasted just as delightful as I'd hoped.

Lily locked her eyes on mine, and her face flushed bright red. I slipped my tongue into her depths. She trembled and made the sexiest little gasps. It surprised me that I could bring her so much pleasure, and that made my passion burn hotter.

Her slender fingers slid into my hair, and she ground herself against me. Her legs closed around me and her heels thumped my back, urging me to go faster. I gave her exactly what she wanted.

I'm sure I fumbled around a bit in pleasing her. Eating pussy is a learned skill. I did my best, though, trying to duplicate what I liked and what she had done so well just a few minutes ago. I spread her pussy and licked along her lips, sucking them into my mouth as I went and occasionally nipping at them gently. Her slightly metallic flavor quickly overwhelmed my senses, and I became lost in pleasuring her.

I smiled wickedly, even though she couldn't see it, and began flicking the tip of my tongue rapidly across her clit while I inserted two fingers and rubbed them across her G-spot.

She threw her head back and moaned. "Oh, god! Yes!"

By the time Lily's leg muscles clenched tight around my head and she screamed her first release, I had decided she was the best lover I'd ever had.

To my immense satisfaction, I brought her to three powerful orgasms, refusing to stop. Her pussy became my world. By the time I finally let her collapse, my lips were a bit raw and my jaw was a little sore, but I was ecstatic. For the first time in five years, I was at peace. It beat drawing a royal flush on the success meter.

My body felt warm and loose as I pulled her to her feet. "Come with me."

Her steps were even more unsteady than mine, so I slipped an arm around her waist and helped her to the back of the house.

My bedroom never saw guests; books and knickknacks filled every available flat surface other than my bed, which I hadn't made this morning.

She looked up at me with those captivating blue eyes of hers as she curled onto the soft, green comforter. "Thank you."

I smiled down at her. "No, thank you. I'll be right back."

I staggered back to the living room, locked the door and grabbed the shotgun. Checking the windows seemed to take an eternity.

When I got back to the bedroom, Lily lay sprawled across the covers, just where I'd left her, fast asleep. I leaned the gun against the wall by the nightstand and sat on the edge of the bed watching her. The strain and pain were gone, and she looked relaxed.

She was gorgeous.

I grabbed a blanket from the closet and pulled it over both of us as I lay down beside her. I nudged my arm under her head and cradled her head against my breast. Lily barely murmured as she changed position, still deep asleep. This was what I'd needed all these years—someone to take care of, and maybe to love. Maybe it's what she needed, too. By the time they cornered Latrell, maybe we both would have found a little healing in each other.

UNDERCOVER

Ily Goyanes

The red vacancy sign kept blinking, annoying the hell out of me. I wasn't sure how this was going to turn out, it being my first time and all. To be honest, I was creeped out by the whole thing, though I'd shoot a hole through my foot before admitting it to the other dicks. *A lesbian rookie vice detective going undercover as a hooker...who woulda thunk?* I had to admit though; I felt sorrier for Rick. The only other rookie detective in the department was doing his undercover in drag, three blocks away.

My mom had been a cop, too. A detective actually, homicide. Detective Liliana Garcia, the first Hispanic female to make detective in the Miami-Dade Police Department. She was the one who instilled in me the need to go after real criminals, the murderers, the child molesters, the rapists. And the politicians, of course. Mami would tell me how much time the MDPD wasted going after poor schlubs who committed victimless crimes like smoking a joint or giving a $20 blow job, only to have gangbangers roaming the streets, free to rape, steal and kill. But there I was, ready to bust some lonely, sex-deprived john who had to pay someone to keep him company. Who was the schlub now, Mom?

The drizzle was tapering off and I was grateful. I had been standing on the street corner for forty-five minutes in a miniskirt and halter-top, and even my bones were cold. The brass had decided the sting should go down in December, of all months, the only month the temperature in Miami drops below sixty. As I bounced up and down to keep myself warm, I hoped that whomever I ended up arresting wasn't married with children. If he was, I'd beat myself up over it all night, even *with* a bottle of scotch for comfort.

A car pulled up to the curb a few feet away from me. It was one of those luxury jobbies, all bright and shiny. I put on my best 'straight' pose, the one that didn't make me look like I'd puke from kissing a guy. The car slowly approached and the tinted window on the passenger side lowered. *Well, this is it, kid, make-it-or-break-it time.*

I sauntered over, or at least what I thought sauntering might look like, and almost tripped in my heels. The only time I wore such instruments of torture was for weddings or funerals. I tried leaning into the car sexily and almost fell.

There was a woman sitting in the driver's seat. Oh, boy. She was about ten years older than me, and lord, was she a looker. I thought she might have been lost, until she spoke.

"Are you averse to offering your services to someone of your own sex?" She had long, natural red hair, bright green eyes and tits so big, they almost touched the steering wheel.

"Most definitely not." Oops. I think I may have answered that out of character.

"I would like to take you to a hotel. For the night, if possible."

"What did you have in mind?" I tried *real* hard to get back into cop/hooker mode.

"We'll play it by ear. I figured we could start with some champagne. The rest will take care of itself. I assure you that I will not hurt you. Unless you want me to."

I squeezed my legs together to keep my clit at bay. My type, and I do have one, is older, dominant women. Did I mention gorgeous? Yeah, gorgeous, older, dominant women. This dame was three for three.

I looked into her eyes and remembered that everything we said was being recorded. I didn't want to bust this lady, unless we were role-playing, but there was no way out of the situation that I could think of. My job was to protect and serve, but I swear, if you asked me who I was protecting and serving at the moment, my mind would have drawn a blank. I had to get her to offer me money for sex in a way that would hold up in court. Usually, the "what did you have in mind" line works for cops, but she easily sidestepped that one. I couldn't be too blunt either; that would be entrapment.

"Are we just going to drink champagne and play Scrabble then?"

"I do enjoy a good game of Scrabble, but no. I thought you could model some outfits for me. And I would pay you. To model."

Oh, she was slick all right. I was supposed to turn a john (in this case, a jane) away if I couldn't get him to solicit me for sex outright. The problem was that this broad had piqued my curiosity. The fact that she was a knockout *and* my type didn't help either. All my instincts were telling me to get in her car, so I did. I would tell the captain later that I felt I could get her to proposition me once we were in the hotel, that I had already been standing on the street for an hour, that I was cold and wet, yada, yada, and blah, blah. And yes, Captain, that is the exact moment that my wire stopped working.

She seemed pleased that I got inside the car. I immediately put one hand on her leg, which she quickly removed. "You are to behave until we are safely inside our hotel room."

I was tempted to place my hand back on her leg, just for kicks, to see if she would get mad, but since I *was* still wired, I decided instead to take the opportunity to scope her out. It seemed like her stems stretched from the pedals all the way to the sunroof. She was voluptuous, unlike newbie lesbians, who think stick figures are attractive. Unfortunately, that's all you meet when you go to bars and clubs, which is one of the reasons why I was single. Women like this didn't frequent my local bar on Ladies' Night Thursdays.

"What's your name?" I asked only because I was getting restless. The fact that I had defied orders was starting to hit me, and hard, but if I had resisted her charms, my gut told me I would have spent the rest of my life regretting it.

"Jane." She smiled, and although I've never seen the painting in person, I would say that it was a Mona Lisa smile, all vague and mysterious.

"Well, I'm Trick," I joked back. She laughed. It was a good laugh, healthy but not too strong, and real, not phony.

All of a sudden I saw the hotel looming large. Holy crap! The Biltmore? It cost a few hundred bottle caps a night just to rent a *closet* at that hotel! I had always wanted to stay there, but not looking like a hooker for christ's sake!

She stopped the car on the street before going up the long driveway. "Reach into the backseat; there is a trench coat you can put on over your clothes. It's been raining, so you won't look out of place."

This dame really thought of everything, just like a good

domme would. I reached into the backseat and pulled on a trench coat that, if the designer were any indication, would cost me about a month's salary. Now, I know we had been followed; that was protocol. The other members of the sting were supposed to ensure my safety. The thing is, I knew that they couldn't get to us once we were in the hotel. A hotel like this wouldn't voluntarily divulge a guest's room number, and my fellow officers wouldn't be able to get a warrant to make the hotel do so. After all, the lady had not committed a crime. At least not yet.

We pulled up to the entrance of the hotel. She told the valet to get her luggage, and he removed two suitcases from her trunk. If the trench coat would have cost me a month's pay, her luggage surely would have cost me two.

A bellhop loaded Jane's luggage onto a cart and waited while we checked in. The hotel staff either recognized her or got paid a lot of money to act like it did, because each one of them bent over backward to please her. Then again, she seemed to bring that out in people. I know I was definitely thinking about bending over.

After she checked us in, we got into the elevator with the bellhop. She managed to position me in the rear of the elevator without me even realizing it. As we rode, she bent over slightly, pulled up her dress and adjusted the strap of her garter belt. I didn't miss that scene and neither did the bellhop. We both kept staring at her the entire elevator ride, and I don't think either one of us was thinking about baseball.

The elevator stopped finally. I was wet from the rain and from all the images swimming around in my head. The funny thing was that I could also imagine my brothers in arms, trying to get information out of the front-desk staff. If I didn't have something better to do, I would have loved to watch that exercise in futility.

All three of us walked into the suite. This place was even fancier than I had imagined. It was huge! There was a living room area, a bar, and a balcony with a panoramic view. There were also a couple of rooms set off from the main area. I'm not into interior decorating, so my description of the suite probably wouldn't help, but a twelfth-grade vocabulary word popped into my mind: opulence. It's amazing what the old noodle can recall when it's inspired. The suite had gold and red everywhere; it looked like a palace. I must have been gawking like an idiot, because I heard the door close and turned around to find that I was finally alone with this magnificent creature. Even though I deal with the worst element of society on a daily basis, I felt scared for a moment.

"Excuse me while I go to the bathroom."

"Young ladies do not excuse themselves of their own accord. They ask for permission."

"I'm sorry, ma'am. May I please be excused? I need to use the bathroom."

She looked me up and down, taking her sweet time. "In a moment, you may." She grabbed me by the back of my neck and led me to the suitcases. "Open the one on the right."

I did as she asked. The suitcase had an assortment of lingerie in different colors and bottles of lotion. She grabbed one of the bottles, opened it, sniffed, then held it under my nose. "Do you like this scent? I think it becomes you."

The lotion smelled delicious, like a cross between lavender and fresh peaches. "Yes, ma'am."

She then pulled out a burgundy-colored teddy, held it against me, looked at my face and then down at the teddy. She thrust the teddy and the bottle of lotion into my hands. "Take these into the bathroom with you. Take a bath and put both of them on before you come out."

I started walking toward a door that I thought would lead to the bathroom.

"Trick." I heard that pretty laugh again.

"Yes, ma'am?" I answered.

"Take your time. I'm sure you are still wet and uncomfortable from being forced to stand out in the rain. There is no hurry. You *are* mine all evening, correct?"

"Yes, ma'am." I appreciated her generosity, but I was in no mood for a leisurely bath. I wanted to kiss her plump wet mouth and hold her large breasts in my hands. I had literally risked my career to be with this amazing woman, and I wasn't going to waste any time.

As soon as I got into the bathroom, I removed the wire that had been taped to my chest hours ago and drowned it in the sink, making sure it could never be resuscitated. I drew a bath and threw some complimentary bath crystals in it. Why not? I washed myself, making sure to clean all my parts extremely well, rubbed the lotion into my skin after drying myself off and then threw the teddy on. I stared at myself in the mirror. Although I was somewhat of a tomboy, I did clean up well. I had always kept my hair long—it just made life easier—but I was lean, to the point of looking athletic, which gave my appearance a bit of an edge. I don't know what the teddy was made of, but it felt really smooth on my lotion-soft skin.

When I stepped out of the bathroom, Jane was standing on the balcony in a black corset and black panties with a matching garter belt and stockings. She was sipping a glass of champagne. "Pour yourself a glass and come here."

I wasn't a champagne kind of girl, more beer and scotch really, but I did as she asked. Something made me want to obey her. I joined her on the balcony, slightly shy in my teddy now that I had an audience.

She turned to me. "You look radiant." She motioned her drink toward mine and we clinked glasses.

"Luminous, really. You should step outside your safety zone more often."

I became even shyer at her description of me. I wasn't any of those things. I was a 32-year-old female vice cop, but it was sweet of her to say so. "Thank you, ma'am."

After we finished our champagne she tossed our glasses over the balcony, placed my hands on the railing and stood directly behind me. I looked out at the vast space behind the hotel. I could make out an Olympic-size swimming pool, a golf course and darkness. Then I felt her hands. She had started caressing my shoulders and was languidly trailing her hands across my neck, back, arms and ass. I was on fire for her, and I wondered if she could feel the heat burning inside me.

She moved my hair to the side and started kissing my neck while firmly kneading my ass. I was glad she had placed both my hands on the railing, because without support, I might have made a fool of myself.

"Are you enjoying yourself?" Her voice had changed. It was huskier and less authoritative, as if she had been drinking scotch.

"Yes. Thank you." It was an effort to get the words out. She reached around and cupped my two breasts. I could feel her palms and fingers through the thin fabric of the teddy, and I was sure she could feel my nipples harden at her touch.

"I'm glad. You deserve a night off from work." I heard her laugh again, but like her voice, her laugh had also changed. It was lower and breathy, more like a deep chuckle than the sweet, tinkling laugh I heard earlier.

My body was pressed against the balcony railing, and Jane was pressed against me. She started rubbing my erect nipples through the fabric while kissing my back, shoulders and neck gently. She kissed me with her mouth open, and I could feel her warm tongue on my skin. My breathing was fast, and I started to moan. "Do you want me?" she asked.

"Oh, god, yes." I answered. "So much, ma'am."

She pushed my legs open with one of hers and started rubbing the top of her thigh against my cunt. My hands tightened on the rail for support and I almost came. "Not yet, darling; only when I allow you to." Jane had complete control over me and she knew it.

Her words made me almost come again, but I held it in for her, to please her as she was pleasing me.

One of her hands made its way from my breast to the back of my neck, and she pushed my head forward until I was nearly bent completely over the railing. Her other hand trailed off my breast and down my back before stopping between my legs. "Do you want this?" Jane whispered. "Do you want me to fuck you?"

I could barely stand at that moment, much less speak. I had never been with someone so glamorous, so exciting. She was all I had ever wanted but had never been able to find at any of those girl bars. She was my fantasy come true: a powerful, decisive woman who could turn a tough vice cop into a submissive little girl.

"Yes, ma'am." I used all my strength to give her the answer I knew she wanted. I felt her fingers push inside me, and I used all my willpower not to come without her approval. It felt incredible to be penetrated by her, to know that this stunning woman, dolled up from head to toe in expensive black lingerie, wanted to fuck *me*, a simple public servant. I pushed back onto her hand, wanting her completely inside me, needing to be filled by her perfectly manicured fingers.

She released my neck only to grab a fistful of my hair and

hold me in place, pounding her fingers in and out of my pussy, fast and hard. I could feel my cunt soaked and dripping, and knew that soon I would not be able to hold off the orgasms that were threatening to come, with or without permission.

"Please…"

"Please what?"

"Please, please…"

"You know what you must say. I will not allow you release until you ask correctly."

"Oh, God…please ma'am, please let me come."

"That sounds like a request, not a question."

My pussy ached from the amazing cunt-fuck she was giving me. I was dripping all over her hand and my thighs. I wanted to come so badly, why was she torturing me like this?

"Proper young ladies ask for permission from their mistress. They do not make requests," she reminded me.

Thank you, god. Perhaps she had taken pity on me. "Ma'am, may I please come?"

"You may."

The multiple orgasms rocked my body so hard, it was a surprise I didn't knock us both to the floor. She kept her fingers deep inside me the entire time, which made me come even harder. I continued to hold on to the railing as orgasm after orgasm ripped through me, forcing me to shake violently against her, but she held on the entire time without removing her fingers from inside my cunt.

Once I had stopped shaking, she led me to the king-size bed. The sheets were soft, yet crisp at the same time, the pillows like giant marshmallows. She poured herself more champagne and held it up to my lips so I could drink. We were both lying on the enormous bed, Jane in her black lingerie, and me in the wine-colored teddy. My body was starting to recover from the incredible fucking she had given me. I turned and asked if I could kiss her, but instead she grabbed me by the hair and pulled me close. We started kissing as violently as she had just fucked me, and my clit immediately reignited.

After a few minutes, she pulled her face away from mine. "Remove my panties and service me."

She didn't have to order me to eat her cunt, since it was the only image running through my head. I moved over her neck and her corset, kissing my way down her body. I must have removed her panties too fast, because she told me to slow down. "Yes, ma'am. I'm sorry, ma'am."

Once I was in position and staring at her striking pink cunt, I pressed my face against it and inhaled. Her pussy smelled sweet and she was as wet as I was, her juices pouring from between her legs and over my face. I licked around the outside of her cunt, at the fold between thigh and crotch, and she whimpered. I kissed and nibbled her inner thighs, near her cunt, hearing her moan and feeling her shiver. I was enjoying this just as much as the fucking she had given me, and I hadn't even gotten started on the entrée yet.

She grabbed hold of my hair again and guided my face. "Eat my pussy. *Now.*"

I started licking and sucking her labia and clit like I was getting paid for it. Well, technically, I was.

As I licked her pussy and she became more and more wet, I began to feel the waves of an orgasm making their way through her body. Her thighs tightened on my head, and her body began to lift from the bed. I clamped my arms around her legs to hold her down and began furiously sucking her clit, then gently biting it, circling with my tongue slowly, then flicking my tongue rapidly. She was moaning so loudly and shaking so much that I knew I was giving her what she deserved. If only I could receive a commendation for this! I slowed down to make her wait for it, but she gripped my head in both hands and ordered me to continue. She started rocking her hips back and forth as if she were fucking my face and then erupted into a skull-rocking orgasm that almost threw me off the bed.

After she had finished coming, she pulled me up to her and started kissing me gently, licking and sucking my lips and tongue slowly, tasting herself. Her body continued to tremble against me.

"That was very good, Detective." I froze for a minute. What? Did I hear her correctly, or was my brain so fucked (literally) that I was hearing things? Then she chuckled and spoke again. "You must be very good at what you do. You figured out exactly how to service me without being given any clues."

Was she from Internal Affairs? Was I going to get fired? Screw it. It had been worth it.

She kissed me again deeply. "Relax, Detective. You aren't being reprimanded. Not yet, anyway, but I'm sure your superiors would like a few words with you for not following proper procedure."

I looked at her silently for a minute. "Who are you?"

"My name is Kate Fellows, and I am the CEO of Roundtable Publishing. We own your city's daily newspaper, along with about 300 others across the country. One of our editors wanted to write a piece on the prostitution sting, denouncing it as a waste of taxpayer dollars when you have so many other, more serious, crimes in Miami. The article would have alerted the public to the fact that there were going to be undercover cops posing as prostitutes. There were some legal questions involved."

I wasn't sure what to say, but my brain must have kicked into detective mode. "All your little speech tells me is how you found out about the sting. What were you doing cruising the streets, trying to pick up a hooker?"

"Curiosity, mainly. I wanted to see what a cop dressed as a hooker would look like. I wanted to know if I would be able to tell the difference. "

"That still doesn't tell me why you tried to pick me up."

"I picked you up because I wanted to have sex with you. Plain and simple. No mystery to solve, Detective."

"Did you know I was a cop?"

"Not at first, but once you leaned into my window I knew you were interested in me and experiencing an ethical crisis of your own. To act on your desire and go against departmental procedure or to try and... What is the term? Oh, yes. Bust me. Your internal struggle was all over your face, which excited me even more."

She trailed her hands along my shoulders and sides, looking at me earnestly. "There is nothing for you to be upset about, Detective. You didn't let on that you were a police officer, and I didn't let on that I already suspected you were. We're even."

I thought about what she said. Being a detective and the daughter of a detective, what really bugged me was that I hadn't figured out that she wasn't an ordinary Jane.

She kissed me and I kissed her back. Then I heard that soft, throaty chuckle again. "Now, then. Aren't you supposed to carry a pair of handcuffs?"

RIDING
THE RAILS

Sacchi Green

Hey, Jo! Josie Benoit!"
That voice from my past went all too well with the Springfield Amtrak station, visible through foggy windows and blowing snow. I'd gone to college not far from here, and so had the voice's owner.

"If it isn't Miss Theresa," I grunted, and kept on tugging at the sheepskin jacket caught behind a suitcase on the overhead rack.

"I never forget an ass," Terry said pointedly, casing mine as I reached upward.

"Sure as hell wouldn't have known yours." My jacket finally yielded. I tossed it across the voluptuous décolletage of my seated companion.

A few minutes earlier Yasmin had been whining about being cold. Now, of course, for a new audience, she shrugged off the covering with an enthusiasm that threatened to shrug off her low-cut silk blouse as well. Not that it had been doing much to veil her pouting nipples.

Terry, brushing snow off her shoulders and shaking it from

her hair, rightly accepted my remark as a compliment. Four-teen years ago she'd been on the lumpy side; now she was buff, and all style: sandy hair lightened, cropped, waxed just right; multiple piercings on the left ear and eyebrow, giving her face a rakish slant; studded black leather cut to make the most of the work she'd done on her body.

I'd have felt mundane, with my straight black hair twisted up into a utilitarian knot and my brown uniform not ironed all that well since my last girlfriend had taken off, if I ever gave a damn about appearances. Which might have had something to do with why she took off. Which had a whole lot to do with why I hadn't got laid in two months and wasn't finding it easy to resist Yasmin's efforts.

"You just get on?" Terry asked. "Didn't see you in the station. No way could I have overlooked your little friend." Her eyes raked Yasmin, who practically squirmed with delight.

"Been on since White River Junction," I said shortly. It was more than clear that Terry expected an introduction. "Yasmin, Terry O'Brian. We were in college together. Terry, Princess Yasmin, fourth wife of the Sultan of Isbani." It was some satis-faction to see Terry's jaw drop for an instant before her suave butch façade resurfaced.

"Ooh, Terry!" Yasmin warbled, jiggling provocatively. "I didn't know Sergeant Jo had such nice friends!"

"The princess somehow…missed…leaving New Hampshire with her husband's entourage," I said. "They'd been visiting her stepson at Dartmouth. I'm escorting her to D.C. to rejoin them." As far as I could tell, it had been a combination of Yasmin's laziness and the head wife's hatred that had culmi-nated in Yasmin's missing the limo caravan and her absence going unnoticed until too late. I was developing a good deal of sympathy for the head wife.

"The weather's too risky for flying or driving," I added, "but the train should make it through. Not supposed to be much snow south of Hartford."

"Well, now," Terry said, sliding into the seat facing Yasmin, "I'll be happy to share security duty as far as New York."

"Don't get too happy." I sat down beside my charge. There were suddenly more limbs between us than could comfortably fit. I tried to let my long legs stretch into the aisle, but that tilted my ass too close to Yasmin, who wriggled appreciatively against my holster. I straightened up. "This is official business. The last thing I need is an international incident."

Why the hell hadn't I told Terry to fuck off in the first place? Did I hope she'd distract Yasmin enough to take off some of the pressure? The tension had been building all morning. Even the subtle, insistent rhythm of the train had been driving me toward the edge. Or maybe it was just that the little bitch was too damned good at the game, and too clearly driven by spite. I don't have to like a tease to call her on it, and if I hadn't been on the job I'd have given Yasmin more than she knew she was asking for. If it left my conscience a bit scuffed, what the hell; other parts of me would have earned a fine, lingering glow.

But I was on duty. She was doubly untouchable, and knew it. Seven more hours of this was going to be a particularly interesting version of hell.

"Keep it professional, Jo," Lieutenant Willey had said. "This one's a real handful."

I'd noticed. Several handfuls, in fact, in all the right places, with all the right moves. "Don't worry. I know better than to fuck the sheep I'm herding."

She should have slapped me down for that. Instead, she rolled her eyes toward the door. I saw, too late, that the troublesome sheep had just come in. No chance she hadn't heard me. Anger sparked with interest sharpened her kittenish face, segueing into challenge as she looked me up and down.

"You're off to a great start," the lieutenant said drily. "Just bear in mind that the Sultan wants her back 'untouched,' and I'd just as soon not have to argue the semantics of that with the State Department." Something in her usually impassive expression made me wonder whether our charge had come on to her. If so, I was sure sorry I'd missed it.

By the time the train crossed from Vermont into Massachusetts, I realized that Yasmin would come on to any available pair of trousers, no matter what filled them. Even the professionally affable conductor got flustered when she rubbed up against him in passing, and she had a threesome of college boys so interested that I'd made the mistake of laying a proprietary arm across her shoulders and shooting them my best dyke cop look as I yanked her back to our seats. The look worked fine, but it encouraged Yasmin to renew her attack on me.

"Ow!" she yelped when I tightened my grip on a hand that kept going where it had no business. "Why you are so mean to Yasmin?" Her coquettish pout left me cold, but a definite heat was building where her hand had trailed over my ass and nudged between my thighs. She knew I wasn't impervious.

"Let's just stick to getting you back to your husband," I said neutrally, aware of the continuing interest of the college kids three seats back. The less drama here, the better.

Terry's company, whatever the complications, might be better than being alone with Yasmin. Unless my competitive instincts reared up and made it all exponentially worse.

Terry could have been reading my mind. "Gee, Jo," she said, "remember the last time you introduced me to one of your little friends?" Her grin was demonic.

"How could I forget? You healed up pretty well, though."

I stared pointedly at the scar running up under her pierced eyebrow.

"Nothing like a dueling scar to intrigue the ladies," Terry said cheerfully. "You seem to have found a good dentist."

"You bet." I flashed what one girlfriend used to call my alpha wolf grin.

Yasmin was practically frothing with excitement, jiggling her assets and leaning toward Terry to offer an in-depth view of her cleavage and a whiff of her insistently sensuous perfume. When she balanced this position with a far-from-accidental hand high on my thigh I realized that all I'd done was set her up to try to play us off against each other.

"So, Terry," I said, firmly removing the fingers trying to make their way toward my treacherously responsive crotch. "What are you up to these days? Still living in the area?"

"I'm a paralegal in Northampton," she said. "Going to law school nights." Her gaze lingered on my badge, and for a rare instant I was hyperconscious of the breast under it. "Funny how we both got onto the straight side of the law."

"No kidding," I said. "I'd heard that anything goes in Hamp these days, but can you go to court rigged out like that?"

"I could, but I don't." I was pleasantly surprised to see a bit of a flush rise from her neck to her jawline. "I'm on my way to New York to do some readings at a bookstore in the East Village. And a bit of...socializing...afterward."

"You're a writer?" My surprise was hardly flattering, and her jaw tightened, even as the flush extended all the way to her hairline.

"On the side, yeah," she said brusquely. "Doesn't pay much, but the fringe benefits can be outstanding."

"Hey, if the stories match the get-up, I'll bet they are! Erotica groupies, huh?"

Terry caught the new respect in my voice, and relaxed. She let her legs splay apart. I'd already noticed she was packing; now Yasmin stared at the huge bulge stretching the black leather pants along the right thigh, and her kewpie-doll mouth formed an awe-struck O.

"Loaded for bear, aren't you," I said. "Ah, the literary life. I'll have to check out some of your stuff, maybe get you to autograph a book for me." I was more than half serious. She started to grin, and then an odd, startled look swept over her face. I glanced down and saw Yasmin's stockinged foot nudging against the straining black leather.

It wasn't a big enough deal to account for my first, raging impulse to break her leg. I managed to suppress it, but by then everything seemed to be happening in slow motion except the throbbing in my crotch. Terry's presence was definitely making things worse. Much worse.

Yasmin pulled her silk skirt up so we could get the full benefit of the shapely leg extended between the seats and the toes caressing the leather-sheathed cock. Then she applied enough force that Terry caught her breath and automatically shifted her hips to get the most benefit, and I felt the pressure as though it were prodding against my own clit. But all I was packing was a gun, and that was on my hip.

I know from experience that you don't get the optimum angle the way Yasmin was working. But you can get damned close. My girlfriend used to tease me like that in restaurants, her leg up under the table, her foot in my lap, her eyes gleaming wickedly as she watched me struggle not to make the kind of sounds you can't make in public. She knew I wouldn't let myself come, because I just can't manage it without a whole lot of noise.

The train wasn't crowded, but it was public. Terry's head

was thrown back, her eyes glazed over, her hands gripping the seat hard. I was afraid my own breathing was even louder than hers; I was damned sure my cunt was just as hot and wet. I had to stop the little bitch, but I was afraid if I touched her I'd do serious damage.

Then Yasmin, with a sly sidelong glance at me, unbuttoned her blouse and spread it open. She fondled her own breasts, and her rosy nipples, which had thrust against the silky fabric all morning as though permanently engorged, grew even fuller and harder. Her torso undulated as her butt squirmed against the seat. Her foot was still working Terry's equipment, but her focus had shifted to herself.

"God*damn*!" came Terry's harsh whisper. Or maybe it was mine. Then Yasmin turned slightly and leaned toward me, still working her flesh, offering it to me, watching my reaction with half-closed eyes, her little pink tongue moving over her full upper lip. The tantalizing effect of her perfume was magnified by the musk of three aroused cunts.

"We're coming into Hartford." Terry's strangled words sounded far away. "We'll be at the station any minute!"

Yasmin's voice, soft, taunting, so close that I felt her breath on my neck, echoed through my head. "Sergeant Jo doesn't have the balls to fuck a sheep!"

I snapped.

I lunged.

With my right hand I clamped her wrists together above her head. With my left arm across her windpipe I pinned her to the seat back. I leaned over her, one knee between her thighs. Then I dropped my hands to her shoulders and began to shake her so hard her head bobbled and her tits jiggled against my shirtfront and the hard edges of my badge.

A strong hand grabbed my shoulder and yanked me back.

When I resisted, something whacked me fairly hard across the back of my head. Then a soft, bulky object—my sheepskin jacket—was shoved down between us.

"Damnit, Jo, cool it!" Terry gritted. "And you," she said to Yasmin in a tone slightly less harsh, "you little slut, and I mean that in the best possible sense of the word, cover up, or I'll let the sergeant toss you out onto the train platform."

I nearly turned on her, but people were moving down the aisles to get off the train, and more people would be getting on. By the time the train was rolling again I'd begun to get a grip, although I was still breathing hard and my heart, along with several other body parts, was still pounding.

"Thanks," I muttered. "Guess I needed that."

"What you need," Terry said deliberately, "is a good fucking. Jeezus, Jo, if you don't get off pretty damn soon you'll have not only that international incident, but the mother of all lawsuits!"

She was right, which just made things worse. I glanced at Yasmin. She had stopped whimpering and sat clutching my jacket around herself, watching us with great interest.

I pushed myself up into the aisle. "Can I trust you to keep her out of trouble for a couple of minutes while I at least take a leak?"

"You can count on me," Terry said, and I had to go with it.

There was a handicapped-accessible restroom just across from us, long and roomy by Amtrak standards. I pissed, tied my long straggling hair back up as well as I could and leaned my pelvis against the edge of the sink. It was cold, but not enough to do me any good. Then I shoved off and unlocked the door, knowing that nothing I could do for myself would give me enough relief to be worth the hassle.

As the door slid open a black-clad arm came through, then a

shoulder, and suddenly Terry and Yasmin were in there with me, and the door was shut and locked again.

"Sudden attack of patriotism," Terry announced with a lupine grin. "Have to prevent that international incident. It's a tough job, but somebody's gotta do it."

"You and who else?" I challenged.

"Just me. Our little friend is going to keep real quiet, now and forever, in return for letting her watch. No accusations, false or otherwise."

I looked at Yasmin. Her eyes were avid. "On my mother's grave!" she said, and then, as I still looked skeptical, added, "On my sister's grave!" Somehow, that was convincing. Just the same I unhooked the cuffs from my belt and snapped them around her wrists with paper towels for padding, then pinned her to the door handle. When I turned back to Terry, the quirk of her brow made me realize my tacit agreement. To what, I wasn't sure.

We sized each other up like wrestlers considering grips. Then Terry made her move, trying to press me against the wall with her body, and I reflexively raised a knee to fend her off. Her cock against my kneecap made feel naked. I'm used to being the hard-body in these encounters. I know the steps to this dance, but I've never done them going backward.

She retreated a few inches. "Gonna stay in uniform?" she asked, eyeing my badge. I unpinned it, slipped it into my holster, unfastened my belt and hung the whole deal on a coat hook.

"Civilian enough for you?"

"Hell, no! The least you could do is show me your tits."

I stared her in the eyes for a second—somehow I'd never noticed how green they could get—and started to unbutton my shirt. I wasn't sure yet just where I might draw the line, but I could give a little. "Fair enough." I hung my shirt and sports bra over the gun and holster, even yanked my hair loose from its knot and let it flow over my shoulders. It would have come down anyway. "How about you?" She had left her jacket behind but still wore a tight-cut leather vest over a black silk shirt.

Terry was observing me with such interest that she might not have heard. "Breasts like pomegranates," she said softly. "Round and high and tight. Geez, don't they have gravity in New Hampshire?"

I looked down at myself. My nipples were hardening as though under an independent impulse; I could sure feel them, though. I grabbed Terry's vest and pulled her close to mash the studded leather hard against me, then eased up just enough to rub languorously against it. The leather felt intriguing enough that I didn't push the issue of her staying dressed.

Terry pressed closer again. I leaned my mouth against her ear. "Pomegranates? Christ, Terry, is that the kind of tripe you write?"

"Yeah, well, maybe when the inspiration's right. But then I edit it out."

She eased back and looked me over again. "I don't suppose," she said, somewhat wistfully, "you could jiggle a little for me?"

"In your dreams!" We were both a little short of breath by now, both struggling with the question of who'd get to do what to whom. Much as my flesh wanted to be touched, my instinct was to lash out if she tried.

"In my dreams?" There was such an odd look in her eyes that I didn't notice right away when she raised her hands until they almost brushed the outer curve of my breasts. "In my dreams," she murmured, just barely stroking me, "you're wearing red velvet."

I hadn't thought of that dress in years. Maybe the last one I ever wore. She'd worn black satin. A college mixer, some clumsy groping in a broom closet, a few weeks of feverish euphoria;

then the realization that instead of striking sparks we were more apt to knock chips off of each other. Eventually, in fact, we did. I ran my tongue over my reconstructed teeth.

Terry telegraphed an attempt at a kiss, but I wasn't quite ready for that. I did let her cup my breasts and rub her thumbs over the appreciative nipples. "One time only offer," I said, "for old times' sake," and pulled her head downward. She nuzzled the hollow of my throat while I ran my fingers through her crisp brush cut. Then she went lower, her open mouth wet and hot on my skin, and by the time she was biting where it really mattered, her knee was working between my thighs, and I was rubbing against it like a cat in heat.

"Come on," I muttered, "Show me what you've got." I groped the bulge in her crotch, and then, while she unbuckled and unzipped and rearranged her gear for action, I kicked off my boots and pants.

She tried to clinch too fast. I let her grab my ass for a second, then grabbed hers and shoved those tight leather pants back far enough that I could get a good look at what had been pressing between my legs.

"State of the art, huh?" Eight thick inches of glistening black high-tech cock, slippery even when not yet wet. I'd have been envious any other time. Hell, I was still envious.

"This one's mostly for show," she muttered. "Are you sure…" But it was too late not to be sure.

"I can handle it," I said. And I did handle it, working it with my fingers, making her gasp and squirm. I manipulated it so that the tip just licked at me, then leaned into it, and for long seconds we were linked in a surreal co-ownership of the black cock, clits zinged by a current sweeter than electricity but as sharp. Then the slick material skidded in my wetness and slid along my folds, and I spread for it and took it in just an inch or two.

Can't hurt to see how the other half lives, I thought, and then, as Terry pressed harder, I remembered the size of what I was dealing with and realized that yeah, it might hurt, and yeah, I might just like it that way.

She pulled back a little and thrust again, and I opened up more, and she plunged harder, building into a compelling rhythm. I gripped the safety railing behind me and tilted my hips to take her deeper inside, hungry for the pounding, aching intensity.

But I needed to go after it myself. "Let me move!" I grated.

Terry, uncomprehending, resisted my attempts to swing her around, and the black cock, glistening for real now, slipped out as we grappled together. "What the..." Her voice was guttural, and her eyes glittered dangerously.

We were pretty evenly matched in strength. She was a bit beefier; I was taller. She'd been working out with weights and machines; I'd been working over smartass punks and pot-bellied drunks. The tiebreaker was that I needed it more.

"You get to wear it; just shut up and let me work it!" I had her back against the rail now. I grabbed the slippery cock and held it steady just long enough to get it where I needed it and then began some serious action.

For an instant she flashed a grin, and muttered "Fair enough!" Then she did all she could do to hang on to the railing and meet my lunges. The train swayed and rattled, but I rode it, my legs automatically absorbing the shifts, as I rode that black cock, train to my tunnel, bound for glory. The hunger it fed and compounded got me so slippery that in spite of its size, the impact and friction might not have been enough, except that my clit seemed to swell inward as well as outward, and my whole cunt clenched around the maddening pressure.

Terry's grunts turned into moans. She grabbed my hips and dug her fingers into my ass. "Steady...damnit...steady..." I slowed enough to catch her rhythm and grabbed her leather-covered ass, feeling the muscles clench and her hips start to buck. I mashed my mouth down over hers to catch the eruption of harsh groans, but she had to breathe, and anyway, it didn't matter how much noise she made. I could feel my own eruption coming and knew there was no way I could muffle it. And I didn't give a damn.

I held on until Terry's gasps subsided from wrenching to merely hard. Then I accelerated into my own demanding beat. I saw her face through a haze, and there may have been pain on it, but she didn't flinch, just kept her hips tilted at the optimum angle for me to ram myself down onto what she offered. My clit clenched like a fist, harder and harder each time I drove it onto her pubic bone. A sound like a distant train whistle seemed to come closer and closer, the reverberations penetrating into places I hadn't known I had.

Then it hit. My clit went off like a brass gong, and those waves smashed up against the explosion raging outward from my core. Sound engulfed me.

Terry held me for the hours it seemed to take for me to suck in enough breath to see straight. Finally I slouched back against the edge of the sink, letting the slippery cock emerge inch by inch. She reached past me to grab a handful of paper towels. I took them away from her and slowly, sensuously wiped away my own juices from the glistening black surface. When I aimed the used towels toward the trash container she stopped me, folded them inside a clean one, and tucked them into her waistband, avoiding my eyes. I didn't ask.

Then she looked over toward the door. I'd been vaguely aware at one point of Yasmin, one hand pulled free of the cuffs I'd fastened too carelessly, rubbing herself into a frenzy; apparently, by her look now, with some success. "So, Princess," Terry said with the old jaunty quirk of her brow, "didn't I tell you it'd be worth it just to hear her come? I could record that riff and make a bundle."

"You, Terry, are a prick," I said lazily, "and I mean that in the best possible sense of the word."

"I still get the shivers now and then," Terry went on, nominally speaking to Yasmin, "thinking of that alto sax wailing fuller and fuller. The final trumpet fanfare this time, though, was beyond anything I remember."

"Jeez, I hope you edit out that kind of crap!" I said, and turned to the sink to clean up. Then I dressed, and felt more secure with my gun belt around my hips. Not that security is everything.

The rest of the trip wasn't bad. Yasmin watched sleepily as Terry and I chatted about old times, old acquaintances, and the intervening years. Terry got off at Penn Station, offering me a book at the last minute with her card tucked into it; she grinned when I took out the card and slipped it into my breast pocket, behind the badge.

"Moving a little stiffly, aren't we," I said as I helped Terry get her duffle down from the rack.

"Mmm, but the show must go on."

"I'm sure you won't disappoint your audience," I said, with an encouraging slap on that fine, muscular ass. "Go get 'em."

Yasmin made a few tentative advances between New York and DC, but I wasn't vulnerable anymore, and she gave up and slept for most of the trip. The welcoming party at Union Station was headed by a tall, mature woman in a well-cut dark suit. "The Princess traveled well?" she asked, with a keen, hard look at me.

"Just fine," I said, meeting her eyes frankly, "with no harm done, if you don't count a few slaps to make her keep her hands to herself."

"Excellent," she said, with the ghost of a smile. "The Sultan would be happy to offer hospitality for the night, before your return trip."

"I appreciate the offer," I said truthfully, "but I have other plans. I'm getting the next train back as far as New York. There's a literary event I don't want to miss." Terry's schedule of readings had been scrawled on the back of her card. There was a special private one at midnight. I had a notion there'd be enough erotica groupies to go around. Beyond that, I wouldn't mind meeting an editor, finding out more about the writing game. I knew damned well that Terry would use some of today's activities in her fiction. I might just beat her to it.

I've gotta edit out that "train to my tunnel, bound for glory" line, though. Too bad. That's sure as hell exactly how it felt.

BLAZING JUNE

J. L. Merrow

It's been a proper scorcher for this early in June, and the air's thick with pollen as they break into Mrs. MacReady's. I feel like a spare part, hovering by the front door with its telltale pint of semi-skimmed sitting in a little puddle of dried-up spilled milk. If only I'd been here earlier to see it.

"Is Mrs. Mac going to prison?" Billy asks.

"No, love!" I pick him up, though he's getting too big for that really. "The police are just going in to make sure she's all right, seeing as she wasn't answering her door."

"What if she's out at the shops? Won't she be cross they've broken her window?"

"Mrs. Mac only goes out on Saturdays, when the taxi calls, remember?" He's too heavy, so I put him down before I do myself a mischief. But I keep my arm around him. "Is she all right?" I ask the male constable when he comes out again.

He gives me a smile. "Don't worry. We've called an ambulance, but I think she's just a bit dehydrated, that's all. Still, won't hurt to get her checked out."

"Did she have another fall?" I feel guilty for asking.

He nods, but he's got my meaning. "Happened before, has it? How did she manage then?"

"She's always been able to pass me a key through the letterbox, and I go in and get her back on her feet." More and more often, these days.

"Let me guess—won't trust anyone with a spare key?" The constable shrugs, like he understands what old people are like. It's a bit of a relief. "We'll have to contact social services, get her assessed. See if they think she's up to looking after herself."

I've got a fair idea how that'll go, and I feel guilty again. But it's for the best, isn't it?

"She smells funny," Billy puts in.

"Billy! What have I told you?" I turn back to the constable, and now the WPC's there, too. "His dad's a tactless old so-and-so too," I say apologetically.

The Woman Police Constable is about my age, probably, though I expect most people would say she looks younger. She's got pale red hair, a sort of golden color, cropped close so when she turns her head you can see short, feathery hair at the nape of her neck. It looks soft, like velvet. Her skin's creamy-pale, and she's got a sort of lean grace to her even under all the kit the police seem to wear these days. Makes most policewomen look dumpy, but not her.

She's got a handkerchief or something wrapped round her hand, and I realize with a jolt she's bleeding. "Are you all right?"

She shrugs, and smiles. It's a nice smile. "Cut myself on the window. I'll live."

"Let me look at it for you. At least wash it out." My eyes dart over to Mrs. MacReady's front door, with its peeling paint and grimy net curtains over the broken windowpane. She gets the point.

"Thanks. That's very kind of you. Mark, you're all right staying with Mrs. MacReady, aren't you?"

The constable wrinkles his nose, but he goes in anyway.

"I'm Ellen, by the way," she tells me as we step across the landing and into mine, and I realize what a god-awful mess I left it in this morning.

"Carla," I say back. "And this is Billy, my little monster."

She grins. "I'm sure you're not a monster really," she says to Billy, but he goes all shy and hides behind my legs. "Must be a bit crowded for three of you, in a flat this size."

"Oh, I'm not with his dad!" I don't know why I blush. "Never was, to be honest, but VJ's a good dad to Billy. He has him every Friday. That's why I was out all day."

"Making the most of it?"

I nod. "It's my day at the gym—yeah, I know, could do with a few more of them." I carry on quickly, so she doesn't feel she has to say something polite. "Then I do the shopping. No point dragging Billy round Tesco's when I don't have to. But it means I'm out all day, so that's why I didn't notice the milk. Here, you run your hand under the tap while I get the first-aid kit."

"Sounds like you're a good neighbor to the old dear," she says, loud so it'll carry over the sound of running water.

I'm not, really. I mean, I look in on her, and I get stuff for her when she's not up to shopping, but I always feel I ought to do more. "I try," I say.

"Hasn't she got any family?"

I'm back with the bandages. Billy's happy enough watching TV, and I don't feel bad about it, knowing he's spent the day playing footie with his dad. "She was married, but they never had any kids. I don't think she's got anyone, now." I have to concentrate, as I dab her hand dry with a clean towel and then wipe the cut with antiseptic. She's got lovely hands, long, slender fingers with short, blunt nails. Practical. Not like my bunches of sausages with nail varnish that always seems to chip as soon as I put it on.

"Sad, to be all alone like that," she says. "Goes to show, though, doesn't it? I mean, my mum's always on me to find a man and get married, but she did all that and still ended up alone."

"Oh, not you too? That's mums for you. S'pose I'll be the same one day, pestering Billy to give me grandkids!" We both laugh, and I put the dressing on her cut. Slowly, so I don't have to let go of her hand too soon. Daft, really.

"So which gym do you go to?" she asks, not pulling her hand away or anything.

"Just the sports center one. They do a special rate if you're on benefits." I flush. "I mean, VJ gives me what he can, but it's not enough to live on, and by the time you've paid for child care…"

She's still smiling. "I know, believe me. And anyway, what's the point of working just to pay someone else to look after your kid? He'd rather have you, wouldn't he? And who could blame him?" I'm sure she just means because I'm his mum, though her voice is soft as she says it, and she gazes into my eyes like it could mean something more.

There's a knock on the door, even though we left it open. "Ellen? The ambulance is here," the male constable calls.

"I'd better go," she says, as our hands slide apart. I'd like to think there's regret in her eyes. They're pale gray, and beautiful like the rest of her. "Thanks for patching me up."

Next Friday Mrs. MacReady still hasn't come back to her flat, and I wonder if she ever will. I hope she doesn't hate me for calling the police. I've been in that flat, with its bare floorboards and crumpled newspapers; I know all she had left was her independence.

I go to the gym as usual, and it does the trick, like it always does. I don't know if it's the exercise or MTV, but when I'm in there it's like another world: no worries, just thoughts. I think about Ellen, but it's not a sad kind of longing like it has been all week, just a gentle happiness that I ever met her.

And then I see her. She walks in like a dancer, all cool and sporty in her Nike pants and vest top, so slender they drape as much as they cling. She smiles when she sees me on the exercise bike and comes over to say hello. I'm horribly conscious of my faded breast cancer T-shirt and the saggy jogging bottoms I got for two quid down the market.

"Hi, Carla! I thought I'd give this place a try—my gym costs a fortune, and it's not all that great. Maybe we could have a coffee, afterward?"

I pant out a yes, and she smiles again and goes off to the elliptical. It's dead ahead of me, and as she moves I can see her hips outlined, see that lovely heart shape of her bum. Her arms are pale, like the rest of her, and a little muscled, but still soft-looking.

I do an extra ten minutes on the bike without even noticing.

I'm just wondering how much longer I can string out my usual routine without making it obvious when she comes over. She still looks as cool as a spring morning, even with her face a little pink from the exercise and beads of sweat on her chest. I try not to stare at those. I must look a right state, all red-faced and panting.

"I'm ready for my shower, now—are you nearly done?" she asks, like she doesn't know.

"Yeah, I think I'll call it a day, too," I say, and we walk down to the changing rooms together.

My breathing isn't getting any slower, and it has nothing to do with how fit I'm not.

I wonder how she managed to get a locker so close to mine. Maybe it's luck. Maybe someone up there does give a fart about me after all. We park our bags on the same bench, hers all smart and with a label, mine a battered old knockoff that's falling to pieces but still just about doing the job. "You know, I like it here," Ellen says, pulling off her T-shirt. "Think I might get a membership."

She's got lovely breasts, I see, as she struggles out of her sports bra. Small and perfect, with the prettiest pink nipples you ever saw. Me, I have to stand well back when I take my bra off so I don't take her eye out with one of my big bazoombas. Stretch marks on them, too, not that anyone's got close enough to notice in a good long while.

"You know, when I was at school I'd have killed for a bust-line like yours," she says.

"We should've traded bodies," I tell her. "I always hated everyone looking at my chest."

"Can't blame them, though, can you?" She pulls off her Nike pants and the thong beneath, and I can't think of anything to say. She's so beautiful. So pale and willowy, like a dryad or a naiad from the stories my mum used to tell me when I was little. The hair at her crotch is darker, like ginger snaps. I wonder if she tastes as sweet. She smiles. "I'm just dying for a shower, aren't you?"

And she grabs her towel and a couple of bottles, and pads off to the showers in her bare feet, and I just stand there with my tits out, open-mouthed.

Then I finally get my arse in gear and follow her.

* * *

She orders a latte in the cafe afterward, and I have a cappuccino. "Have you heard anything about Mrs. MacReady?" I ask, because it's been preying on my mind.

Ellen nods. "'Fraid so. She won't be going back to the flat. They'll find her a home. I'll let you know where."

"Thanks. I'd like to visit her." If it's not on the bus routes, maybe VJ would give me a lift, instead of to the gym on a Friday. "She's not really got anyone else." I'd like to spoon up the chocolaty froth from my cappuccino, but I don't want Ellen to think I've got no manners. Then I catch her watching me playing with my spoon with a wicked look in her eye, and I do it anyway. Her smile makes my stomach flutter.

"I think she's like us," I say. "Mrs. MacReady. I mean, she's never said so, but she told me once she only got married because she wanted kids. And then she never had any. How bloody awful is that?"

"Things are better now," Ellen says, picking up her spoon and a packet of sugar. "We've got choices she never had."

"What's it like, being a policewoman?" I ask.

She shrugs. "Oh, I dunno. What's it like being a mum?"

"It's brilliant," I tell her. "Best thing I ever did. Don't know what I'd do without my Billy, even if he can be a bit of a so-and-so sometimes. It's just—you know how relationships, sometimes they don't last? But your kid, he's yours for keeps." I go a bit red, I think. "I don't usually go on about it like this, though."

Her eyes seem to sparkle. "You should do it more often, then." She stirs her coffee, then takes out the spoon and holds my gaze as she gives it a lick before putting it on the saucer. "I always knew it'd be either the police or the army for me. Decided in the end I wasn't sure if I could actually kill anyone, if it came down to it, so the police it was."

"I bet your family is proud of you." I don't mean it to come out a bit wistful.

She just smiles again. "Oh, you know families. Never satisfied. So, you and Billy's dad, how did that happen?"

It usually hurts, when anyone asks that. And it's not that it doesn't now, but somehow, this time it's more like I'm feeling the memory of it, rather than the pain itself. "I never meant to be a single mum. I was in a relationship, had been for a couple of years, when I started trying for a baby. But when I miscarried, she couldn't deal with it. It was like she thought it was a judgment on us or something." Or maybe she just wanted an excuse. "But when she left, I still wanted a baby. And that's when VJ said, look, there's not much chance he'd be having a kid any other way, why didn't we have one together?"

"So you did. It must have been hard." Her hand brushes mine.

"Worth it, though," I say, and then I have to take a sip of my coffee because my throat's gone dry.

Ellen tells me she's got the day off, so we spend it together. Daft stuff, like walking through the park and getting ice cream. She likes vanilla; I've always gone for chocolate. They're a good mix, together. When we get back to my place, she asks if she can come in. I wish I'd tidied up, but it's not like she hasn't seen the mess before. There's an old film on BBC2 so we sit down to watch it, but halfway through she slides her arm around my shoulders. I don't mean to make so much of it, but when I turn in surprise it just seems natural to kiss her.

She tastes sweet, and her lips are cool and soft as ice cream. I kiss her again, worried she's going to melt away from me. Her hand comes up to cup my boob, and it's like there's a direct line sending the tingles straight down to my crotch. I'm wet for her already. I shuffle closer on the sofa, and she throws a leg over mine so she's sitting on my lap, the film forgotten, and her hand still kneads my boob. I push up her T-shirt. Her skin's like velvet, with steel underneath. I don't think I've ever wanted anyone this badly.

Ellen breaks the kiss to lean back and tear off her T-shirt. I wish I had the courage to do the same but I'm not like her. I'm not beautiful, me.

Ellen does it for me, and then she undoes my bra and kisses my boobs like they're something special. "You're lovely," she says, so sweetly, so breathily I almost believe her. I can't speak, so I unhook her bra and set those perfect breasts free. Her nipples pucker and harden, so I tongue them gently to encourage them. She gasps and arches her back. Then she climbs right off me to undo her jeans and slide them down those slender hips.

I never knew what a turn-on it could be to have a beautiful, naked woman on my lap while I'm still half-dressed. From the waist down I'm perfectly respectable, at least to the naked eye, although from the waist up I'm a wanton slut. I grab her bottom, kneading the cheeks and pulling them apart.

"How long have we got?" she asks, her voice rough.

I look at the clock and work it out. Takes a bit longer than usual. "Couple of hours yet, before VJ brings Billy back."

"Then take me to bed."

"You go first," I say. I want to look at her as she walks, all fluid motion wrapped up in smooth, creamy skin. There's a tattoo of a rose on her left cheek, where only a lover would see it. I brush it lightly with my fingertips as she walks, and she shivers.

"I want to see all of you," she says when we get there, her hands on my hips, then sliding up to my boobs. I undo my jeans and push them off awkwardly. At least I've got decent undies on. I never wear my worst ones when I go to the gym.

"Take those off too," she says. "I'm busy."

She is, too, kneading my boobs and brushing her thumbs over my nipples, making them stand out proud. I step out of my damp knickers, and she drops to her knees, kissing her way all down my belly. My legs shiver as she nuzzles into my crotch. "Lie down," I tell her.

"Only if you do, too." She smiles and stands up, putting her arms around my waist. We kiss again, all tongues and hands, then climb onto the bed, still kissing.

I slither down, about to go down on her. "No," she says. "Come back, I want to see your breasts." So I use my hand on her, and she plays with my boobs, licking and sucking and biting them as she gets close. She feels like molten gold around my fingers, and when she comes she arches her back and cries like a cat. I stroke her as she comes down from it. I still can't believe she's here with me.

"Your turn," she says, and kisses her way all down me, her face still flushed and her eyes bright as diamonds. She's got a wicked tongue on her, Ellen has. It teases as much as it pleasures, keeping me on the edge so long I think I'm going to die. When I fall, I shatter, but she's there to pick me up again and hold me.

Afterward, we lie together on the sheets, basking in the warmth of the afternoon sun, the duvet thrown to the floor. Ellen's head is on my shoulder, and one hand's just playing with my boob.

"Going to miss these when you leave?" I ask. It doesn't come out as light as I'd hoped.

"I'm going to dream of these, love," she says with a smile in her voice. "Mind you keep them safe until I come round again. When can I come round again?"

Any time, day or night, but I'm not so daft as to say it. Well, maybe I am, at that. "Come whenever you can," I say.

Ellen sighs into my breast. "Wish I could say tomorrow, but I'm on lates. Shift work's a sod."

"I'm a mum, remember?" I say, pulling her closer. "I'm used to broken nights. Come when you can."

I feel her smile against my skin, and I close my eyes on the sunlight streaming through the curtains, making the dust motes dance and sparkle for joy.

June's never blazed so bright.

A PRAYER
BEFORE BED

Annabeth Leong

N echama swung herself up out of the police car and surveyed the scene. A homicide was adding insult to injury in a neighborhood like this, the violence of one person against another like a boot grinding into the wounds of poverty that God had already inflicted on the people who lived here.

The place was swarming, caution tape bright yellow against the faded gray paint of the two-family home. Uniformed personnel of all shapes and sizes trampled the weeds that overran the yard, which had probably gone neglected because neither of the families living in the building had decided whose responsibility it was.

Nechama glanced back to her new partner, Tom. The expression on his clean-shaven white face was all business, and she needed to be the same. Maybe she could blame the pressure of his naïve enthusiasm for justice; whatever the cause, Nechama had been feeling old. She needed to pull it together fast, before they went inside. A suspected domestic violence case—one where the boyfriend had likely strangled the girlfriend and then slit her throat—would have plenty of horrors waiting in the interior. This was no time to get sentimental about the front lawn.

As usual, the rhythms of the job calmed and prepared her. She checked that her badge and gun were in place and tucked in a few of the coarse, tawny curls that had escaped from the severe bun trying to restrain them. She took comfort in the sensation of her powerful muscles as she strode alongside Tom to report in and get briefed on the status of the scene.

"Zayden, we need someone to take a statement from the neighbor who found the body," the supervising detective told Nechama. "She's been watching the victim's kids, but Junior here can take over while you talk to her."

"Yes, sir."

Nechama gestured with her shoulder for Tom to follow. She pushed through the crowd of forensic scientists examining the doorframe at the mouth of the house and allowed herself a quick glance up the stairs, where the body still lay. Then she motioned toward the door to the apartment to the left.

Tom knocked, giving Nechama a chance to observe. She saw the telltale signs of her partner's nerves. His index finger persistently flicked at a nonexistent spot on his pants, and he worked his jaw as if chewing gum.

The door opened. The neighbor was a petite black woman, her skin so dark that the whites of her eyes glowed like streetlights at midnight. Even wearing sweats, she carried herself like she was worth $7 million. Her head was shaved close, and she wore big, gold, hoop earrings decorated with feathers. Her body rippled with compact muscle. Her eyes were hostile, her jaw set and her posture challenged either of the cops to just try fucking with her. Somewhere behind her, a kid was crying, and another set of kids were giggling hysterically.

Mostly, Nechama didn't think about sex while on the job. It was never appropriate and often a dangerous distraction. This time, she couldn't help imagining herself sliding down those sweats, her own shaded Sephardic skin light against the deep hue of the other woman's legs.

The woman blinked sharply at Nechama, seeming to read her thoughts. Nechama dropped her eyes, clearing her throat to signal Tom.

"Sorry to bother you, ma'am," Tom said. "We need to take a statement from you."

She put both hands on her hips. "And who's going to watch all these kids?"

"Um, that would be me." Tom flicked again at his pants then stuck out his hand. "I'm Officer Tom Phillips. My partner, Nechama Zayden, will be the one talking to you."

"Officer Phillips, with all due respect, have you ever held a child in your life?"

Nechama braced herself for trouble, but Tom surprised her. "Seven years as a camp counselor, certifications in CPR and first aid, and I was most of the way to a degree in social work specializing in dealing with young children before I changed direction and became a cop."

Nechama barely held back an exclamation of surprise. The witness was just as taken aback. She opened her mouth, closed it again, then stepped out of the doorway and gestured Tom inside. She watched him walk down the hall, and Nechama felt an irrational flicker of jealousy. Then the woman squared her shoulders and turned her attention fully to Nechama for the first time.

"You can come inside, too, Officer Zayden."

"Thank you." Nechama hesitated, feeling for a moment as if she were on a first date. She held out her hand. "I apologize, but I never caught your name."

"Marleen Williams. Come inside."

Nechama couldn't resist staring at Marleen's ass as she led the way into the kitchen and poured coffee for both of them. Marleen didn't so much walk as stalk. Her every gesture suggested a simmering, sensual anger that made Nechama want to unwrap her and unwind her secrets.

"Ms. Williams," Nechama said after a moment. She forced her eyes higher as Marleen turned around, just managing to meet her gaze despite a distracted moment staring at her full lips. "I'm sure this is a difficult situation for you, but I'd like to make a recording of you talking about what you've seen today. I'm walking into this cold, so I'll ask you to keep that in mind as you describe what's happened."

Marleen nodded, but her eyes stayed wary. Nechama got out her digital recorder and placed it on the table between them. Marleen set down coffee cups for both of them, the liquid almost as black as her skin. Nechama usually took cream and sugar, but she didn't feel she could ask.

Marleen sat at the table, and her face got even harder. "The upstairs neighbor's name is Chantel. We watch—watched—each other's kids sometimes. I try not to leave mine with her—too many different men up in there, and too much liquor. But sometimes. Anyway, last night, I was sitting up late after I put my two to bed. I heard a thud." The woman paused, scrubbing at her face with the heel of her hand.

"Can you describe the thud?" Nechama prodded.

"Heavy. Loud. Horrible. It was like I already knew what it was. I didn't really know. But I walked to the spot under where it happened and waited there. I heard footsteps coming down the stairs. I thought about opening the door." Marleen stopped and shook her head. "I didn't want to. I didn't go to sleep after that for a long time."

"About what time was this?"

"Maybe around midnight? Then in the morning, little Sean comes knocking on my door. He says his mommy's sleeping on the kitchen floor, and he can't get her up."

"What did you do?" Nechama said.

Marleen took a long drink of her coffee. Nechama tried hers. It was so hot that she thought Marleen must have burned her mouth and throat, though she showed no sign of pain.

"I told him to go away," Marleen said finally. "Told him we were all tired with damn kids driving us crazy, and it was a Sunday morning, and the good Lord made a day of rest for a reason. He came back three more times, and I kept sending him away. But the last time, I was lying there thinking about that thud again, and the next time he came, I let him in. I made him eat a bowl of cereal with me before I would go upstairs to help him."

"And what did you see when you went upstairs?"

Marleen slammed her coffee cup down on the table, causing some of the burning liquid to splash out and onto her hand. She didn't react. "What do you think I fucking saw? I saw Chantel's dead body on the kitchen floor."

Nechama blinked and cleared her throat. "I'm very sorry for what you had to see, Ms. Williams," she began.

"Are you?" Marleen challenged. "I'm not like you. I don't get excited dealing with these situations."

"Ms. Williams, I do this because I want to help people, not because I get excited."

"Really?" Marleen's hand darted out and pinched Nechama's left nipple. Nechama had to bite back a yelp that would have been equal parts surprise and arousal. She jumped up from her chair, one hand on her gun.

"You're going to shoot me now?" Marleen said. "I saw your little nipples getting hard when I was talking to you."

Nechama glanced helplessly at the voice recorder. There was no way she wanted audio from the last minute playing in court. "Ms. Williams, I'd appreciate it if we could focus on taking your statement. Your testimony could be very important to finding the person who did this to your neighbor. What you or I feel about it really doesn't matter compared to that, does it?"

Marleen gave a sharp nod, leading with her chin, lowering her hands into her lap.

Nechama stopped her current recording and queued up a new one. It felt unethical to erase the embarrassing one, but she could try to set things up so it was easy not to play it in court. She kept her eyes off Marleen altogether, choosing a spot in the middle of the table. Her left breast felt like Marleen had burned it. She was so aroused, her nipple almost stung. She took a deep breath. "Now, I think we're going to need to start over."

"Officer Zayden, would you say that Marleen Williams cooperated with investigating personnel?"

Nechama didn't like the way the defendant's attorney was sneering at her. She shifted uncomfortably in the witness box. Thank god she was able to show up in uniform to testify—if she'd had to change into a dress, she wouldn't have had a prayer of thinking straight.

"She did," Nechama said.

"Did she say or do anything hostile toward you or any of the other officers?"

Nechama hesitated. "Not that I can recall."

The attorney grinned. "Officer Zayden, I'm about to play back what I think is a puzzling interaction with a key witness. Would you like to explain anything about it before I do?"

The prosecutor finally stood up. "Objection, your honor." *About goddamn time*, Nechama thought. Unfortunately, the objection didn't do any good. The defense attorney was trying to discredit Marleen, and the judge deemed it relevant to point to the incident with Nechama as a possible sign of mental instability. Nechama wished her skin were as dark as Marleen's— she'd never felt so on the spot while on the stand, and she was sure that even her relatively swarthy skin wasn't enough to hide her blush.

By the time she got off the stand, she had no idea what had been done to the prosecution's case and barely any memory of what she had actually said. One male juror was leering at her. As she stepped down and made her way out of the courtroom, he winked. Nechama felt her blush intensify, and she dropped her eyes.

Once in the hallway, she made her way straight to the bathroom. She stepped inside, closed and locked the door behind her. Only then did she realize she wasn't alone.

Marleen Williams sat hunched in a corner under the sink, tears streaming down her face but no sound coming out of her mouth. Shoving aside her own feeling of humiliation, Nechama dropped to her knees beside the other woman. "Ms. Williams, are you all right?"

She returned a hostile stare. Nechama just waited a moment, until the other woman spoke grudgingly. "Does it fucking look like I'm all right?"

Memories of the defense attorney's grin were all too recent for Nechama. "Fine," she said. "Forget I asked."

Marleen scrubbed angrily at her face. "Wait, Officer Zayden. I'm sorry. I know none of this is your fault."

"You're damn right it's not," Nechama said.

"I don't want to be here. I didn't want to testify. I don't want to think about this. I never wanted to see it." Tears began to flow again, but they didn't affect Marleen's low, unsettlingly calm voice. Her eyes seemed governed by an entirely different set of laws and emotions than the rest of her body. "I didn't ask for this. I didn't ask to be psychologically evaluated. I'm not a criminal."

The singsong litany showed no sign of abating. "Ms. Williams," Nechama said. "Ms. Williams. Marleen." The other woman finally looked up at her first name.

"What do you want from me?"

"I meant what I said. I want to help you." Cautiously, Nechama moved a little closer. She didn't think talking with Marleen Williams would compromise the trial. They'd both testified already. In any case, it was too late to stop now.

Nechama touched the back of the other woman's hand, as lightly as she could. She was close enough to smell Marleen's perfume, a spicy, food-based scent. It soured Nechama's stomach a bit now, layered over the other smells in the bathroom.

Marleen flipped her hand over and grabbed Nechama's, hard enough to hurt. Her fingernails dug into Nechama's skin. "What do you want?"

"I told you." Nechama tried to pull back, but the other woman's grip was iron.

"I don't think you're telling the truth." Marleen pulled her closer in. With her free hand, she grabbed the back of Nechama's head, winding her fingers through the coarse curls there and yanking her head back. She kissed Nechama with a hard mouth, teeth cutting lips, tongue prying Nechama's jaw open, breath forcing into lungs. Nechama was too startled to close her eyes, and she saw Marleen's cold triumph when she couldn't help letting out a moan.

Still controlling Nechama's head with a fistful of hair, Marleen pulled Nechama back. Nechama tried to stay calm, but her breath was coming in a mix of panicky gasps and aroused moans. Marleen flicked at each of Nechama's nipples. "Think I just gave you a little of what you want."

"Why are you doing this? Maybe I...maybe I did want you when I saw you. That didn't mean I was going to make a move or do anything unfair to you."

"That's what they all say," Marleen said, jerking Nechama's head for emphasis. "Going all the way back to Daddy and Uncle Jefferson and all the way up through Mrs. Pontin senior year of high school and Jeff Wainwright, career counselor, and Miss Maura Pembroke, loan officer at the local bank." Marleen's fierce eyes were rimmed with red.

"Jesus," Nechama said. The revelation killed her arousal for the moment. "You thought I was going to make you do something with me before I'd be willing to do my job?"

Marleen stared back. Nechama pulled herself free of the other woman's grasp. She got up in a kneeling position. "Now, you listen to me," she said, her voice low and strong. "I'm a damn good cop. I'm not about to take advantage of anybody. If you want help from me, all you have to do is let me know. You don't have to put out for me, and you certainly don't have to humiliate me. Are we clear?"

Slowly, Marleen nodded.

"Now, do you need something from me?" Nechama said. "Because otherwise, I'm going to walk out of this bathroom now."

The moment stretched. Nechama sighed and turned away. Before she could get to her feet, Marleen grabbed her again, this time by the wrist. Her hand was like a claw as she pulled Nechama closer. Nechama's pulse began to pound, the chemicals in her body flickering between repulsed adrenaline and mind-bending awareness of the other woman's shape, smell and skin.

Then Marleen fell against Nechama's chest, tears flowing

fast, snot running from her nose. She wrapped her arms around Nechama's waist and clung. For a moment, everything fell into place and Nechama held her, feeling the noiseless sobs wrack the other woman's body.

"I never wanted to see, I never wanted to see, I never wanted to see," Marleen repeated.

"Of course you didn't," Nechama said. "No one does. It's a terrible thing to see." She hesitated, then began to stroke Marleen's back.

"I haven't slept a whole night through since I heard that thud coming from the ceiling," Marleen continued. "Every time I close my eyes, all I can think is that I'm the one lying on the kitchen floor, with my kids around wanting to wake me up." Marleen paused for a moment, looking up at Nechama. "How do you do it? How do you go to sleep at night? You must be seeing this all the time."

Nechama sighed. "Every night before I go to bed, I light a candle and say a blessing for everyone who's on my mind. Then I get in bed and pull the sheets up around me and say the Shema. It's a Jewish prayer. My mother always told me that if I said it before bed, nothing could come and hurt me in the night. Then I close my eyes and do my best."

"I try to say the Lord's Prayer," Marleen says, "but I don't know if I believe God is protecting me."

Her eyes were wide and, for the first time, innocent. Nechama thought for a moment of the children she'd never had, the people she'd never let herself love. She thought of the ways she'd lost faith, and the ways she kept trying.

"You know why I became a cop?" Nechama said. She never told this story to anyone, not the real story. There was no stopping the wild impulse that drove her forward now. "I found my mother dead when I was eleven. The cops who came weren't very nice to me. I think they were too shocked to be nice. She looked terrible. You know why I say the Shema every night? It's because I thought she must have died because she forgot to say it. Even after I stopped believing that, I couldn't stop saying the prayer. I wanted to be a cop because I wanted to make sure there was someone nice around to talk to the kids, and to the other people who are affected by what's happened."

"You never stopped seeing her," Marleen said. "You never learned how to go to sleep."

Nechama swallowed. "Yeah. I guess that's right."

"Did you hear what happened with the Costas case?" Tom said. He was driving the car on patrol. His tone was casual, but Nechama saw how his jaw worked and his knuckles whitened as they gripped the steering wheel. "The guy got off."

"Yeah?" Nechama said. Her tone was the same. It was funny how they needed to play this game with each other, she thought. As if they were actually going to fool someone. "I thought the evidence against the guy looked pretty good."

"It looked good to us," Tom said. "We know what evidence usually looks like. Damn juries these days have been spoiled by 'CSI.' They won't find someone guilty unless forensics finds a fingerprint complete with DNA, name, and signed confession."

Nechama snorted. Then she sobered. "Marleen must be taking this pretty hard."

Tom leered. "First name basis now, is it? You'd know whether she's been taking it hard. How hard have you been giving it to her?"

"Shut the fuck up."

"Seriously, you should have cuffed her when she grabbed you. Assaulting a police officer. Would have made the whole thing look less suspicious. They still would have had to throw out her testimony, but the incident wouldn't have added to the defense attorney's argument that 'the cops mishandled the situation.'"

Nechama looked out the window. It was a fierce summer day. Everyone walking by on the street looked like they were barely keeping themselves upright under the heat. "Tom, I tell you what. You advise me on how to do my job when you've got a couple more years in, okay?"

"Both you and Marleen are 'children of trauma,' huh?"

She snapped her head left to look at him. "What the hell are you talking about?"

"We studied it in the psych courses I took for my social work degree. Even as adults, children of trauma tend to form twisted alliances with each other. Misplaced loyalty, keeping secrets, it's all part of the pathology."

"Thanks, Tom," Nechama said. The sight of his overearnest expression made her sick. "Send the bill to my home address, okay?"

Nechama resisted the urge to park her car around the corner and walk to Marleen's front door. She didn't have anything to hide, she told herself. She wasn't doing anything wrong.

She hesitated outside. The peeling gray house paint seemed on the verge of revealing the building's bloody insides.

Nechama took a deep breath and went in the front, turning left to knock at Marleen's door.

"What the hell do you want? Am I a suspect now?" Marleen said. She looked like she'd just come home from work. She wore a black pencil skirt, a rich brown silk blouse, an architectural pair of gold earrings and peep-toe ankle boots. But the hot day must have gotten to her, because Nechama could smell her body even from several feet away.

"Ms. Williams," Nechama began, then stopped. They had to be way past last names after the nipple tweaks and kissing and crying. "Marleen. I just wanted to see how you're doing. I know they didn't treat you well on the stand, and I heard the defendant was acquitted."

Marleen shrugged. "I never expected it to be fair." She cocked her head to the side and her face softened slightly. "You on duty right now?"

Nechama looked down at herself. The ever-present uniform almost seemed part of her skin. "No. I probably should have taken this off before coming out here."

"It's all right. You want some coffee?"

"Yeah. I would." Nechama couldn't help flicking her eyes up and down Marleen's body again. Everything about the other woman—her eyes, her nails, her words—seemed sharp and designed to get deep inside of Nechama.

"I can't promise I'm going to behave like a sane and reasonable person," Marleen said.

"Is that the line the defense attorney used on you? He's a prick."

Marleen smiled and led Nechama inside.

"Where are the kids?" Nechama said.

"Their grandma is watching them for a while. I'll go over to see them in a bit. I didn't want them staying in this building. The doctors said they didn't understand what happened, but I think they did."

Nechama nodded. She noticed details of the house more than she had last time. Marleen liked big, bold colors and wild pieces, but she had only one such thing in every room. Nechama couldn't help looking up at the ceiling.

"You can still hear the thud, can't you?" Marleen said.

"Have you thought about moving out?"

"Yeah. I have to save for first, last and security deposit, but believe me. I've thought about it."

Marleen poured coffee. "It's fresh," she said. "I put it on as soon as I got home." Nechama sat at the table. The familiarity of it all had her reaching for her voice recorder, bracing herself for the horrors that waited upstairs. She shook her head, realizing she was picturing her own mother up there, not Chantel Costas.

"What did you say to your kids?" Nechama said. "Since you think they understood what was going on?"

Marleen's smile was bitter. "I taught them a prayer," she said. "I told them that if they say it before they go to bed, nothing will come and hurt them in the night."

Nechama stared at her. She reached out across the table and took the hand that came to meet hers there. The gesture had been instinctual, but as soon as they touched skin to skin, fire ran up and down her veins.

"Officer Zayden," Marleen said.

"Nechama."

"Right. I'm sorry about the way I've been to you."

Nechama shrugged. "I didn't—"

"No. Let me apologize."

"You shouldn't have to. I was looking at you that way. I wasn't going to do anything about it. It wasn't a requirement before you could have my help. But I did like the way you touched me."

Nechama looked at their hands, still linked on the table. She blinked back sudden tears and fixed her eyes on Marleen's stove. The dark hand that gripped her cheek and turned it was delicate, firm and callused. Though Marleen was the shorter one, she pulled them both up and sucked Nechama into another of her hard kisses.

Ever since she was a teenager, Nechama had been the harder one with her lovers, pushing against their softness, bending them to her desire. It was strange and new to open her mouth and let Marleen's tongue inside, to feel the biting empathy of the way the other woman explored her.

Marleen's hands were claws, tearing at Nechama's uniform, opening buttons and armor and, sometimes, skin. Nechama stood shivering, passive for once, letting the other woman reveal her. When she stood naked, Marleen finally took her lips away and stood back.

Nechama looked down at herself. She saw red marks across her breasts and belly, and felt them also stinging across her back. The sight of Marleen still dressed and neat sent a flash of arousing humiliation through Nechama. Marleen reached out and pinched Nechama's nipple hard, digging her fingernails in. Nechama sank to her knees on the tiled kitchen floor.

"You like it like this?" Marleen said.

"Yes," Nechama gasped. "Please."

Marleen let go of Nechama's nipple and grabbed her hair. She stepped closer. Nechama gripped Marleen's legs to keep herself upright, clinging to them through the tears clouding her vision. Marleen pulled up her skirt and yanked Nechama's face against her panty-covered pussy.

Nechama pressed forward and breathed the other woman's strong smell. She found Marleen's clit with her nose and wiggled against it as she licked her red silk panties.

Keeping hold of Nechama's hair, Marleen stepped further forward, driving Nechama to her back on the floor. She settled herself over Nechama's face, trapping her between small but powerful thighs.

Nechama brought her hands up and pulled the panties aside, working one of her fingers inside Marleen's pussy as she sucked her clit into her mouth. Marleen let out small grunts and ground hard against Nechama's face. Her hips wound in a circle, and she pulled Nechama's hair hard enough to keep the back of her head off the floor. Nechama could barely breathe, but the feeling of drowning just excited her more. She worked second and third fingers inside Marleen and kept her tongue moving desperately.

She felt the other woman's thighs tensing as she got close to coming. "Come on," Nechama murmured into her pussy. "Come for me. All over my mouth."

Marleen was gasping and sweating, her pussy clenching Nechama's fingers. Nechama felt her getting closer and closer. Marleen's head tilted back, and her jaws went rigid. Then at the last moment, Marleen whispered a broken "No!" She jerked away from Nechama's mouth, releasing hold of her hair so quickly that the back of Nechama's head crashed against the floor.

Nechama lay panting, still tasting and smelling Marleen. She lifted a hand toward her. "Wait! Why?"

Marleen hugged herself, shaking her head. She paced the kitchen, her skirt askew.

"Come back and let me touch you," Nechama whispered. She held out her arms.

"No one ever makes me come," Marleen said.

"Maybe I'm different."

Nechama was rewarded with the signature hard stare, and then a hesitant step forward. Slowly, Marleen lowered herself to the floor beside Nechama, nestling into her arms. Nechama stroked her back and kissed her forehead. "What you want," Nechama whispered, "is for me to touch you like this. You want me to make you feel good, but you're afraid to let me. Why?"

"It doesn't matter," Marleen said. She rolled onto Nechama and pressed her tongue into her mouth again, chewing on Nechama's lower lip, almost cutting off her air supply. Nechama groaned and arched her hips up. Her body opened under Marleen, softening and moistening. She spread her legs, just in time to receive the fingers Marleen jammed inside her.

Marleen bit and pinched her way down Nechama's body, so that Nechama blinked back tears of pleasure and pain by the time the other woman's mouth arrived at her pussy. Marleen twisted her fingers inside Nechama, spreading them to stretch her, shaping them like a hook and pressing hard against her G-spot. Nechama could smell her own scent filling the kitchen. She'd never been so wet in her life. She ground her heels against the tile and pressed up against Marleen's hand, just as the other woman bit her mound.

Nechama shrieked and came, felt stabbing pleasure as her pussy convulsed around the fingers stuffed inside her. Marleen licked her then, her tongue rough like a cat's but tender, and that soft core inside the painful orgasm made Nechama sob and try to pull away.

Marleen didn't let go, her tongue inexorable and slow. Her hand knew just when to twist to prolong the sensation for Nechama. She didn't pull back until Nechama lay gasping and completely spent.

Nechama reached for her. "Please," she said. "Come here. Please." Marleen didn't respond, but she didn't pull away when Nechama hauled herself up and rolled onto her. She slipped her finger between Marleen's labia, just stroking up and down without particularly trying to stimulate her.

Nechama kissed Marleen. It was actually possible to keep her tongue patient now that Marleen had worked her over so hard. She moved her tongue and finger in time—carefully, never urgently. She laid her free hand against the side of the other woman's neck. Every time Marleen began to stiffen, Nechama eased up just a little. Though Marleen's pulse pounded against Nechama's fingers, her body stayed loose.

Then she gave a soft grunt, and Nechama felt the orgasm rippling out of Marleen, around Nechama's tongue in her mouth and Nechama's finger in her pussy. Nechama didn't try to draw the orgasm out or change it. She just soothed Marleen as it happened, petting her neck and kissing her temples.

"There," Marleen said finally, voice hard. "You got what you wanted."

Nechama looked up and saw tears welling in Marleen's eyes. "I hope we both got what we wanted," Nechama said. Her body felt sore and empty, as if her own stabbing orgasm had expelled some old splinter that had lodged deep inside her.

"I don't think anyone can give me what I want," Marleen said, her eyes drifting to the ceiling.

"What's that?" Nechama said.

"I want to be safe."

The words stabbed Nechama's heart. She had wanted that, too. When no one else seemed able to give it to her, she'd wanted to do what she could to make others safe. It was hard not to take Marleen's statement as a personal criticism.

She clasped Marleen against her chest. "Let me help you," Nechama said. "Let me make you safe." Nechama repeated the words and rocked there on the sticky tile. It wasn't just Marleen she was talking to now. She also spoke to her mother, to Chantel Costas, to Marleen's children, to herself. Marleen's small body rested in her arms, filled with heat and anger but pliable for now. There was no forgiveness or softness in her anywhere, Nechama thought, but there might be a seed of hope.

HOW DOES YOUR GARDEN GROW?

Cheyenne Blue

The track was rough enough that the patrol car wallowed in the sandy soil, its sump scraping over protruding rocks. By the time I reached the building at the end, I knew I had several long scrapes on the car's paint from the banksias that crowded the lane and probably underbody damage.

The track ended in a clearing in the trees. The building was not exactly a house, but more than a shed. It was long and low with a veranda running the full length, facing south into the sun. A few chickens pecked their way around the ground, weaving through piles of timber, an old mangle and an ancient Toyota.

I got out of the patrol car and started toward the shed.

"I don't get many visitors. What do you want?"

I turned in the direction of the voice, shading my eyes to the slanting sun. A woman hunkered down on the veranda steps smoking a roll-up. She was weather-beaten and nut brown, wearing a faded singlet top and tattered shorts. Bare toes curled around the wooden step.

"Eve Jarmyn?"

"Yeah, that's me." The woman uncoiled herself and stood, digging small hands into the pocket of her shorts. Even standing on the bottom step, she barely topped my shoulder.

I flashed my badge. "Senior Constable Cole. I'm here to investigate a complaint about a barking dog."

She stopped my hand as I went to put my badge away, studying it intently. Her eyes crinkled in amusement. "A barking dog? What wally complained about that? My nearest neighbor is over a kilometer away."

"This your only dog?" I pointed to the red heeler standing by her side.

"Yeah."

I glanced past her at the shed, wondering if she had a permit to live in it. "Mind if I take a look out the back?"

"Would it make a difference if I did mind?"

I shrugged. "Easier for both of us if you let me take a look."

"Go ahead. I'm not hiding anything."

I flicked her a glance to see if she looked worried. The barking dog was a cover. We'd had a tip-off she was growing dope. Not a commercial concern, just a few plants, but we still had to follow it up. But she was relaxed, smiling slightly. Either she really did have nothing to hide, or she was sure nothing would be found.

I walked around the side of the shed, noting the rough-hewn timber and wide veranda. Indeed, most of the shed was open; there was no wall separating the veranda from the house. I could see a couple of couches, a long timber table and a kitchen bench top covered with jars of something.

Behind the shed were raised garden beds with a profusion of growth. Heavy tomatoes grew along one side, peas and beans curled over trellises, a forest of basil grew underneath a passion-fruit vine. There was more I couldn't name. If she had dope plants here, they'd be well hidden.

"Quite the gardener," I commented, as I walked between the beds.

Eve followed me. "I grow enough for myself, some leftover to sell." She picked a Lebanese cucumber from the plant and bit into it. She handed me the other half. It was crisp and tasted of sunshine.

Beyond the vegetables there was a cleared patch of ground and then the rainforest started abruptly, palm trees and thick, lush undergrowth as impenetrable as a manicured hedge. I turned around and started back between a different set of beds. There were eggplant, capsicum, bok choy and many green plants I couldn't name, but no sign of anything illicit.

"No dogs down here," I remarked, remembering my cover.

"No," she agreed. "Just Jaffa."

"I'll need to see the dog license."

"It's in the house." She led the way up the back steps to the veranda. Pots of herbs were clustered about the posts, and there was an old enamel bath sunk into the timber. Maybe she bathed out here on warm summer evenings. I imagined her slim figure lying back in warm water, looking up at the stars.

"Come through." She led the way into the house. As well as the kitchen and couches I'd seen earlier, now I could see a large bed in one corner, rumpled and unmade, and a tiled shower in an alcove. No shower curtain. Either she lived alone or saw no need for privacy.

Eve went over to a corner and rummaged in a drawer, coming back with a crumpled piece of paper. "The last dog rego renewal."

A quick glance told me it was current, but I'd guessed that already.

"Is that all?"

"That's all. I'm sorry to bother you. Obviously the complainant was wrong—you're too far away from anyone for it to be your dog."

"Obviously."

The shoulder of her singlet had fallen down one arm, and she hitched it back absently, but not before I'd caught a glimpse of small curved breast. My stomach tightened in reaction. How long had it been since Renny, my last girlfriend, left? Too long, obviously, if a sun-brown shoulder and a flash of nipple could get me hot under the collar.

I turned on my heel and headed back to the patrol car. "We'll be in touch if there's a problem."

As I bumped my way back along her laneway, I could see her in the rearview mirror. Her long, black plait fell forward over one shoulder as she bent to pet the dog.

A couple of days later, I was heading out from the station for another boring few hours standing beside the highway with a radar gun, when the sarge called after me. "Kaye, one last call for you. You need to go back to the Jarmyn place where you were the other day. There's been another anonymous call about her growing dope."

"I saw nothing except eggplant two days ago." And a nice breast, I added to myself.

Fred shrugged and hoisted his gut higher. "We have to follow these drug calls up promptly. Queensland Government anti-drugs initiative."

"I'll try and get by later."

"Make sure you do."

After three hours beside the highway, I figured that Fred had been insistent enough that I get out to Eve's place to justify shutting the radar gun off a bit early. It was a good twenty-minute drive to her shed, through the hinterland and up a series of dirt roads into the hills. Far enough from the coast that land was cheap and would attract few chance visitors. Perfect if she is growing a plant or two.

I bumped down the track to her house and cut the engine. The dog, Jaffa, ran out to greet me, but there was no sign of Eve. The pickup was still parked out front and the shed was open; the few doors that could shut were wide open to the sunshine.

"Anyone home?" I called. "Police. Routine visit."

Lorikeets chirped in a red gum, but otherwise there was no answer. I stepped onto the creaking veranda and rapped hard on the framework with my knuckles. "Police. Anyone home?"

I walked around to the other side and repeated my call but all was quiet. Perfect. I could take a long look at exactly what was growing in that veggie garden without Eve being any the wiser. Methodically I started down the first row, making sure to part the thickets of beans and look behind.

By the third row, I'd seen more veggies than were contained in the local supermarket. I'd also found some prolific raspberry bushes and guiltily sampled a handful. They were so sweet and juicy that I had another handful, and then another. By the time I'd reached the end of the veggie patch, I'd sampled crisp cucumber, sweet passion fruit, young peas and tiny guava, but there was no sign of anything illegal.

Obviously, this was a wasted trip. Yeah, wasted because Eve wasn't home, my little inner voice responded. Because she's the first woman who's pinged your interest since Renny left.

I turned back to the car, and then I saw a figure sitting silently on the rear steps.

"Find anything?" Eve rose to her feet and ambled over. "Of course not, because there isn't anything to find. Nothing that would interest you anyway."

Her lips twitched, as if she were trying not to grin.

"I called out several times," I said defensively. "You didn't answer."

"I was potting seeds out the back; it's hard to hear out there. I just happened to see you grazing in my veggie patch. The raspberries are good, aren't they?"

Reflexively I wiped the back of my hand over my mouth, and this time Eve did grin.

"It'll take more than that to get rid of the stains."

She moved in front of me. With the sun behind her she appeared ethereal; fine boned, slender, almost fragile as her silhouette softened her outline. Then the illusion dissipated as she moved closer. Now the sun threw firm muscles into relief and spun the fine hairs on her arms into gold.

When had I become this fanciful? I thought in bewilderment. Cops were practical people, hard-edged and brittle, not given to poetic musings about strangers. About suspects.

She moved closer still, into my personal space, and licked her fingers. Cops are taught not to let people get too close, but I fought the urge to step backward, out of Eve's reach. She was no threat—at least not to my physical safety. Carefully, she wiped around my mouth with damp fingers. When she pulled them away, they were stained raspberry red. My skin tingled where she'd touched it.

"That's better," she said. "Evidence gone."

I cleared my throat, desperate to return to my accepted role. I was here on police business and I needed to remember that. Police business, I thought, with an edge of desperation, as Eve touched my hand. Police business. Police busi...

Thought fled as she stretched up and pressed her mouth to mine. Her tongue flickered out to lap at the corners of my lips.

She stepped back again. "Are you going to book me for assaulting a police officer?"

I struggled to find the officious words I needed to put her in her place. Stern words that would put distance between us and wrap my uniform around me once more in an impenetrable shield. I managed a step back, but the hum between my legs wouldn't be ignored.

Eve obviously knew it. Her off-kilter smile was knowing. "Cat got your tongue?"

"We had a tip-off," I began, but she interrupted me.

"I suppose I'm growing dope among my tomato plants? Last week it was the barking dog, this week I'm growing dope. What will it be next week, Senior Constable? Terrorists in my attic? You know, a woman might wonder if you keep coming here for another reason."

"The police have got better things to do than waste time," I snapped. "What reason could I possibly have for coming here other than police business?"

"This," she said, and once again closed the gap between us and stretched up to fit her lips firmly on mine.

This time I was ready for her. I can read the signs as well as the next person, and her interest had shone like sunlight off a tin roof. But while it wasn't a surprise it didn't mean I was going to melt like lemon drops and fall into her arms and heart. There was also the very real possibility that she was distracting me, seducing me away from the dope plants hidden goddess knows where.

I stiffened, grasped her shoulders and pushed her firmly away from me. My lips were warm and damp where she'd touched them. My hands slid away from her shoulders. She had freckles on her shoulders, I noted absently, tiny sun-kisses on her golden skin.

"Don't tell me you don't like women, Kaye?"

"It's not that." She must have remembered my name from my badge. It sounded warm, the way she said it, a long, low syllable.

"So it must be because you're on duty? Unless I'm not your type? Do you like shaven, buffed, prettied women with fake nails and tans? Or gym rats, all ripped abs and singlets? I have the ripped singlet." Her fingers toyed with the tear in her shirt, a small rent, just above one breast.

"Well, Kaye? If you don't want me, you only need say so. Maybe the boys down the station have another dyke they can send down to investigate me."

"Are you always this talkative?"

"Only when I sense the opposition is weakening."

"What about when they've capitulated?"

"Then there's no need for talk."

I vacillated, torn between the desire to slap her down, find some pretext to wipe that smile from her face, and simply giving in. Simply walking over to her, pulling down that loose singlet top and nuzzling my face into her breasts. Finding out what her hair felt like freed from its thick plait, seeing how it would fall over her shoulders, how long it was when loose. I was a breath away from ignoring duty, the reason I was here, the possibility Eve was a criminal—albeit a very minor one.

I just couldn't do it. If she were hiding dope plants, if she were distracting me and I fell for it, my career would be on the line. I'd been a cop for eight years; it was my life, what I loved best. I couldn't throw that away for a quick fuck, albeit a good one.

I rested my hands on her shoulders, stared into her face. She had tiny laugh lines from the sun, a smattering of freckles over the bridge of her nose. Her eyes were golden, warm and glowing. Tiger's eyes.

"One question. Are you growing dope?"

I concentrated on her eyes. Cops are good at reading body language. Any hesitation, a flicker of her eyes to the left, and chances were good she was lying. But her gaze was direct and steady, no infinitesimal shift away.

"No."

I did what I'd fantasized about; my hands slid from her shoulders along her arms, easing down the straps of her top. She wasn't wearing a bra. Her breasts curved gently from her chest, sun-kissed like the rest of her. Her nipples were dark, and there were a few long, golden hairs ringing each one. I palmed them in my hands, feeling how instantly her nipples hardened, pressing against my palms.

Eve shed the singlet and stood before me. Her baggy shorts had a tie at the waist. My fingers moved purposefully down her taut stomach to tug lightly on the string. It gave, and the shorts pooled around her feet.

It seemed she disdained underwear. I'd guessed she'd be *au natural* from the golden fuzz that covered her shins, and I was right. Her bush was luxuriant and dense, wiry brown curls that hid her pussy completely.

I've never been one for the natural look—I like to see what I'm about to get—but with Eve it was different. I wanted to part those curls, probe with fingers and tongue and find her pussy, expose her pink slit, find out how wet she was, what she tasted like on my tongue.

She took my hand, threading her fingers firmly through mine. I expected her to lead me into the cool of her house, away from the bright sunlight, but instead she tugged me down the garden, toward her veggie patch. Her bare feet padded softly over the dusty earth, through the profusion of growth, down to the end of the row, where the raspberry canes tilted in haphazard disarray.

The sun burned hot on my shoulders through my uniform shirt, and my face felt flushed underneath my broad-brimmed hat.

Eve turned and small hands reached up to flick my hat from my head. It spun away, landing neatly on a stake where tomatoes hung ripe and heavy. Her fingers were busy working down the buttons of my blue uniform shirt, efficiently flicking them open, then pulling my shirt from my shorts.

My sports bra was functional, designed for comfort rather than excitement, but Eve didn't seem to mind. She groped around the back, finding the closure with an ease that told me this certainly wasn't the first time she'd undressed a woman.

She leaned forward and kissed each nipple lightly, sucking briefly with moist lips. When she moved away, my nipples were warm and damp with the absence of her mouth.

I found my belt fastening and removed the belt with fingers that were less than steady. Even through the thrum of arousal, I took the time to lay it carefully on the ground. The sun gleamed on the handle of my Glock and the metal handcuffs.

Taking Eve by the shoulders, I led her a pace away, over to where the sunshine dappled through the raspberry canes, and there was enough grass to provide an illusion of softness. With my belt gone, Eve made swift work of my shorts, dragging my panties down with them. I kicked them away and we were both naked.

My breath sucked in at the contrast we made: Eve, petite and golden, compact and lithe with messy hair, and me, tall and gangling with full breasts that made me look stately rather than voluptuous. We sank to the ground together, hands mapping the lines of each other's body.

I love the first time with someone new. As well as the sexual thrill, there's the joy of discovery. Does she like what I'm doing? Is she ticklish? Is she passive or aggressive? Eve, it seemed, was the assertive type. We grappled together on the grass, our lips melded together in a hot, wet kiss that was all teeth and tongues, thrust and parry, advance and retreat as we explored each other. For one so lightly built, she was wiry and strong.

I rolled onto my back, taking her over with me so that she straddled my body. Her thighs gripped my hips, and her lush pubes ticked my skin. She leaned down so that her heavy braid fell forward, tickling my cheek, and pressed down with her weight. She was wet already; I could feel her moisture spreading on my skin as she shifted. I wanted to push my fingers into her pussy and feel her clasping heat, piston my hand inside her, let her feel that delicious sensation of being engorged and full, the sweet ache of excitement. And I wanted to taste her, see if she tasted of sunshine and raspberries and the sharp scents of the Aussie bush.

She moved down my body, and her mouth closed around my nipple. Her hands shaped my breast, brought it up toward her mouth. I closed my eyes, and the bright sunlight shot sparks behind my eyelids. It was all sensation: Eve's mouth on my breast, her pussy sliding damply across my skin, sunlight warming my skin, and the tickle of something small—an ant maybe—running across my leg.

Eve moved lower, shuffling down my body, letting her lips trail a path from my breast down to my bare pussy. I hadn't waxed for a while so there was a fine regrowth, and her lips pressed a gentle kiss on my mound. Then she shifted quickly so that she was between my thighs. She parted me carefully with her fingers; I felt her lips enclose my clit. She sucked gently, and her fingers pushed their way inside me as I'd wanted to do to her.

I needed to touch her, too. Reaching down, I grasped her plait, winding its thick length around my fist, holding her lips where I wanted them. Oh, she was good at this. Not too much pressure, just as I like, a soft, wet suction. With a silent "oh" of pleasure, I started to come, pushing myself into her face, my back arching in a taut bowstring of need. Silent spasms around her fingers, the sweet feeling of fullness.

When I opened my eyes, Eve was still between my thighs. Her lips and chin were wet and shining. I tightened my grip on her hair, tugging until she moved back up along my body.

She realized what I wanted and shuffled forward, poised on strong thighs until her pussy hovered above my face. A sigh, and she settled within my reach. My tongue reached out and I lapped, feeling rough, crinkly hair, and tasting the pungent taste of her pussy juices. I used my fingers to part her lips, delve between. Her hair tickled my chin, even caught in my teeth as I moved closer, but I persevered. I grasped her ass and held her to my mouth.

She kept very still, and it was only the tiny grunts and sighs she made that let me know she enjoyed what I was doing. My tongue ached, and her hairs tickled my nose, but I kept going. Her scent surrounded me, and the ground was hard underneath my back. Somewhere overhead a magpie gargled its liquid song, and cicadas shrilled in chorus before falling silent.

"Harder," gasped Eve, the first word she'd said since I went down on her.

I increased the pressure, scraping lightly with my teeth, some suction, some friction, and then the glorious feeling of a woman flying apart underneath my mouth. Hot and wet, sunlight and sound. The tension drained from my body, leaving me limp and sated underneath her.

She smiled down at me, touching my cheek with a damp finger.

"Hey, you still with me?"

I nodded, savoring the moment.

"Going to book me for obstructing police business?"

"Not yet."

"Good." She moved off me and rose to her feet. Holding a hand out, she pulled me up with surprising strength. "What now?"

I wrapped an arm around her shoulders, feeling the play of her muscles as she leaned into my body. "I need to check the house, ma'am. I have a tip-off something may be hidden in your bed. Do I need a search warrant?"

She leaned her weight against me. "No. You can stay there until you find what you want."

That sounded good to me.

The next day I sauntered into the station with a great sated grin still on my face. Turning the corner with a coffee in my hand, I ran straight into Fred. My coffee splashed, leaving a big stain on my pale blue shirt.

"Kaye, just the person I was hoping to see. How'd you do at the Jarmyn place yesterday? Anything of interest?"

I covered my laugh with a cough. "You could say that. It was definitely very interesting indeed."

And I walked off before he could ask me what I meant.

ABOUT THE AUTHORS

JOVE BELLE (jovebelle.wordpress.com) lives in Portland, Oregon, with her partner of fifteen years and their three children. Her novels include *Indelible*, *Chaps*, *Split the Aces* and *Edge of Darkness*, all from Bold Strokes Books.

CHEYENNE BLUE's (www.cheyenneblue.com) erotica has appeared in more than 60 anthologies including *Best Women's Erotica*, *Mammoth Best New Erotica*, *Best Lesbian Erotica*, *Best Lesbian Romance*, *Girl Crazy*, *Girl Crush* and *Lesbian Lust*. She was once "taken in for questioning" about an incident involving a mysterious bag of green tea and an unregistered Holden.

ELIZABETH COLDWELL lives and writes in London. Her stories have been published in a number of anthologies including *Best of Best Women's Erotica*, *A Kiss in the Dark* and *Lesbian Love 1*, *2* and *3*. "Torn Off a Strip" is dedicated to Becky, who's always a force to be reckoned with.

ANDREA DALE's (www.cyvarwydd.com) stories have appeared in *Lesbian Lust*, *Best Lesbian Romance 2011*, *Lesbian Cowboys* and many others. Parts of "Charity and Splendor" are mostly true, but she's being coy and not going to tell you which ones.

DELILAH DEVLIN (www.DelilahDevlin.com) is an award-winning author with a rapidly expanding reputation for writing deliciously edgy stories with complex characters—whether from dark, erotically-charged paranormal worlds or richly descriptive westerns that ring with authenticity.

R. G. EMANUELLE is a writer and editor living in New York City. She co-edited *Skulls and Crossbones*, an anthology of female pirate stories, and her short stories can be found in *Best Lesbian Erotica 2010*, *Khimairal Ink*, *Women in Uniform*, *Read These Lips 4Play*, *Lesbian Lust* and the online collection Oysters & Chocolate.

J. N. GALLAGHER is currently working on a short story collection of erotic fiction, a full-length erotic novel, and a bunch of other stuff that J. N.'s midwestern parents can never, ever be allowed to read.

ILY GOYANES is a Latina lesbian who lives to learn. She writes about food and culture for the *Miami New Times*. Feel free to email her at ily.goyanes@gmail.com.

ANNABETH LEONG's (annabethleong.blogspot.com) lesbian erotica has appeared on Oysters and Chocolate and in *Girl Crush*. Other erotic adventures include technological erotica in Ravenous Romance's *Experimental* anthology and an erotic retelling of "The Six Swans" forthcoming in *Coming Together: Neat*.

KENZIE MATHEWS works in a small library in rural Alaska. When not writing, she paints landscapes and seascapes and walks her dogs. Her work can also be found in *Lesbian Lust* from Cleis Press.

J. L. MERROW (www.jlmerrow.com) read Natural Sciences at Cambridge, where she learned many things, chief amongst which was that she never wanted to see the inside of a lab ever again. She has had more than twenty short stories and novellas published, including her latest novella, *Pricks and Pragmatism*.

LYNN MIXON (lynnmixon.com) lives in Texas with a loving spouse and a herd of cats.

EVAN MORA is a recovering corporate banker living in Toronto who's thrilled to put pen to paper after years of daydreaming in boardrooms. Her works can be found in *Best Lesbian Erotica '09, Best Lesbian Romance '09* and *'10, Where the Girls Are, The Sweetest Kiss: Ravishing Vampire Erotica, Girl Crush, Please, Sir: Erotic Stories of Female Submission, Spank!* and *Best Bondage Erotica '11*.

R. V. RAIMENT is a writer, novelist and philosopher, born in the north of England, now happily established in London and often found feeding squirrels in St. James's Park. R V's stories can be found at Clean Sheets, at ERWA, in *The Mammoth Book of Best New Erotica 5* and *Cream*. R. V. is also the author of the erotic novel *Aphrodite Overboard*.

TERESA NOELLE ROBERTS enjoys writing about women who love hot women, as evidenced by her publication in such anthologies as *Lesbian Lust, Best Lesbian Romance 2009, Best Lesbian Erotica 2009* and *Lipstick on Her Collar*. She's married to someone in law enforcement and has washed far too many uniforms to find them sexy. The courageous people in them are another story.

ABOUT
THE EDITOR

SACCHI GREEN is a Lambda Award winner who writes and edits in western Massachusetts. Her stories have appeared in numerous books, including seven volumes of *Best Lesbian Erotica*, four of *Best Women's Erotica*, three of *Best Lesbian Romance* and *Penthouse* magazine. She has edited or co-edited five previous lesbian erotica anthologies: *Rode Hard, Put Away Wet; Hard Road, Easy Riding; Lipstick on Her Collar* and the Cleis Press anthologies *Lesbian Cowboys, Girl Crazy* and *Lesbian Lust*.